I0733956

REVENGE
OF THE
RENDER

Books by Martin Wilsey

Solstice 31 Trilogy

Still Falling
The Broken Cage
Blood of the Scarecrow

Solstice 31 Universe

Virtues of the Vicious
Shadows of the Sentinel
The Law of Lumina
Revenge of the Render

The Vampire Conspiracy

Blood Heretics
Blood Sky Dreams *

Short Story Collections

Peck's Halfway
Six Years Out

Anthologies as Editor

Silence of the Apoc
Whispers of the Apoc
The Witness Paradox

forthcoming

Revenge of the Render

of the

Render

MARTIN WILSEY

Tannhauser Press

This is a work of fiction. All characters and events portrayed in this novel are fictitious. Any resemblance to actual people or events is purely coincidental.

Revenge of the Render

Copyright © 2024 by Martin Wilsey
All rights reserved.

v1.0

Paperback ISBN: 978-1-945994-98-2
Hardcover ISBN: 978-1-958321-18-8

This book, or any part thereof may not be reproduced in any form without permission from the author.

Banker Square, a font from FontSite Inc.,
free for commercial and personal use.

Cover created by Rotwang Studios
Edited by Donna Royston
Interior design by David Keener
Vector Scene Separator by Poliashenko
via Deposit Photos

Published by Tannhauser Press
www.tannhauserpress.com

"It was my first courier job. It was my last day as an innocent. I had no idea what was in the case I was delivering. I couldn't imagine you could fit something worth over 250 billion credits in one small case."

— Jade Church, 2672

TABLE OF CONTENTS

Chapter 1: Jade Arrives

The *GIN* 109 was one of the oldest still-functioning ships that still flew the galaxy. It was a perfect sphere just over twenty meters across. A silver sphere. Though calling it silver was an understatement. It reflected 99.9993% of light and radiation on a massive spectrum. It had twelve reactors that powered three FTL drives, even though it only needed one reactor and one FTL drive to function.

When it was created, the galaxy was just beginning to be explored. Those explorers were on their own. So it was built to last.

Most of the ships, like it, had been stripped of their components. More practical ship designs soon made this one obsolete. It should have been in a museum or flying as a collector's yacht.

But this ship belonged to Jade. She salvaged it. And now she was flying it. She would discover its secrets soon enough.

Jade was dozing in the pilot seat on the bridge level. The *GIN* had given her a five-minute warning for the transition back from FTL. She was getting used to it. The nausea was minimal as long as she knew it was coming. She knew that a complete refit of all the inertial dampeners would help. These early models ran really thick.

The transition clock wound down, and she closed her eyes momentarily. Jade swallowed and took a deep breath. She was new at this and gave herself some slack, but not too much.

Jade thought that calling Elba a colony was being generous. There was a single small settlement that was under a typical lattice dome. She estimated it might hold five hundred residents. Maybe. It occupied a large island in the temperate zone of the planet. Elba was 75% water but was marked on the charts as a hazard and dangerous to humans. Native species of plants and animals were categorized as extremely dangerous.

The space station above the settlement was impressive. It was parked at Lagrange point, halfway between the planet and its largest moon. It was big enough to house thousands. Cobb, the new governor of Elba, and the team from Oklahoma Salvage salvaged it. They were in the process of recruiting staff for the colony.

"Elba, this is *GIN* 109 on approach. Transmitting security codes now," Jade said over the comms, trying to sound as professional as possible.

"Could this possibly be the Jade Church I've heard so much about from my underfed friend Cobb? Can I have visual?" a jovial voice with an odd accent asked over the comms. Jade activated the viewer, revealing a giant of a man. Jade had never seen a man so fat.

"You have me at a disadvantage, sir." Jade smiled professionally. "To whom am I speaking?"

The reply began with a deep laugh. "I am Morimoto Hirohito, but you will call me Mori. All my dear friends call me

Mori, and you have just become my favorite. Your eyes suit your name, my lovely. That skinny little man failed to mention the beauty of your skin, the deep red of your hair, or…”

“All right, Mori. That’s enough,” Cobb cut in. “Don’t mind Mori, Jade. He’s like that when he’s hungry. And he’s always hungry. I’ve transmitted the landing coordinates. I’ll meet you on the tarmac. Cobb out.”

Mori had taken the interruption as an opportunity to stuff an entire jelly donut into his mouth in one bite, causing jelly to squirt out onto his heavily stained uniform. He wiped it, making the smear even worse.

“Cobb is a tiny man who is determined to ruin all my fun,” Mori said as a small floating robot tried to clean his uniform. “He does feed me well. So I’ll let him live.” Mori’s face became serious as he added, “Be careful on Elba, Jade, my newest and most favorite friend. Everything on this planet has the potential to… kill you.” He paused again as his jovial demeanor returned. “But the steaks are so very good, my love. You must have one. Promise me, sweet Jade. They are delish, and I want that joy for you, my buttercup.”

“I will,” she promised, realizing that his flirting didn’t annoy her. She knew it was an affectation, but somehow, she wasn’t insulted or harassed by it. He was entertaining her.

She loved flying the *GIN* on manual. The controls were tight, and the ship’s movement was silent and smooth. It floated through the atmosphere like a ghost. Its perfect sphere left no wake or vapor trail. She guided it down so she could fly over the valley’s length. Tall grasses swayed below beautifully in the breeze. Vast herds of bison-like creatures grazed in the grasses.

The colony dome was now visible ahead—the facets of it glinting in the sunshine.

How can this be a hazard?

Half a dozen ships of various sizes and types were parked on the tarmac. She could see where Cobb waited.

As light and quiet as possible, she stopped the *GIN* before Cobb and floated three meters above the ground. A tube deployed from the bottom of the ship and rotated, revealing Jade with a large suitcase.

Cobb approached with a bright smile and extended his hand. "Jade, how was your first run? Uneventful, I hope."

Jade set the case down and took Cobb's hand in greeting. "It was a milk run. Lumina Station was great. I've been there a few times. The new Sec Chief sends her regards with the case."

An assistant approached, dressed in a jumpsuit uniform that matched Cobb's. She was Asian and shorter than Jade, and she collected the case without a word.

"Does she still have that black eye?" Cobb obviously knew the Sec Chief well.

"She does." Jade didn't mention that the Sec Chief seemed relieved to have that case off her station.

A small shuttle took off then, with the assistant and the case that Jade presumed was headed for the space station.

A siren began to wail. Cobb turned away from Jade and barked a command, "Status." His eyes focused into the middle distance, obviously receiving data on his heads-up display.

"Jade, my sweet," Mori said on her ear cuff comm unit. "A ship has dropped out of FTL inside the security perimeter, within the atmosphere, heading for the colony. No transponder. How fast can your beautiful pearl of a ship evacuate, my love?"

"I see it." Jade pointed into the sky. A trail of black smoke was streaking across the clouds. Before anyone could react, it crashed hard, only half a kilometer from where they stood. It was well out in the sea of grass. The explosion was the loudest thing Jade had ever heard. She felt the concussion, and a shock wave soon followed.

"Dammit," Cobb cursed. "Mori. There's fire."

The siren changed to Mori's voice on the public address system. "Warning. Grass fire. Winds are currently blowing to the south, away from the colony. Please proceed to the dome. Smoke at Marker 2 has already reached lethal levels."

"Jade, you have two options," Cobb said quickly. You can take off now or stay and wait for the all-clear. It would help if you had a vac-suit on board. When the grass burns, the smoke is extremely toxic, even lethal."

Jade pointed beyond Cobb toward the crash. "There's someone."

"No one could survive a crash like that, much less the toxic smoke," Cobb said.

"No, look." Jade could see a man walking toward them. His head and shoulders were above the grass. The fire and smoke were blowing away from the tarmac, so they stood and watched. He was carrying something. The wind was at Jade's back, so they were safe for the moment. Jade could see what he carried as he cleared the grass onto the tarmac.

It was a mutilated corpse.

The shredded white coveralls were covered in blood. The head was completely gone, as was one arm at the shoulder, the other below the elbow, and both legs below the knees.

The man approached Cobb, and Jade realized it was not a man but a cyborg. The flesh of half his face was burned away, revealing his metal skeleton and glowing red eye. His clothes were also shredded. He held the corpse up to Cobb and paused.

"Help her…" His voice dripped with sorrow.

Chapter 2: To the Station

"Jade, can you take us to the station?" Cobb asked. "Please."

"Yes, this way." Jade began leading them to the *GIN*. "Hurry. The wind is shifting."

"Don't touch them," Cobb warned as they crowded into the lift. "They are covered in poisonous oils from the grasses. We should wait in engineering. You don't want the mess in the rest of your ship."

"You'll save her," the cyborg said, with a hint of threat in his voice.

"Yes, Ty." Cobb was trying to calm him. He knew him. "She'll be fine. So will you. We're going directly to the hospital in the station."

"We were attacked," Ty said. "An ambush. The Sec Chief was right."

It was then that the thing Cobb called Ty looked at Jade. She withered under his gaze. Fear and threats of violence steamed off him like heat. Irrational terror filled Jade as the lift door opened. Cobb and Ty got out on the engineering level, and before the door could close, she saw Ty rip the chest open on the corpse and jam his hand inside.

She stumbled out of the lift on the bridge. Alarms were sounding, warning of the toxic fumes. Smoke was now surrounding the ship. Once in the pilot seat, she ascended straight up until above the clouds. She slowly drifted her ship over the crash site.

How had anything walked away from that?

The wildfires in the grasses moved at an alarming rate. The bison were stampeding toward the far end of the large island. A large predator species that looked like part lion, part dinosaur, the same color as the grass, and the size of a horse. They stalked the bison and seemed immune to the fire and toxic fumes. The slower beasts climbed the rocks to escape the flames, only to find these Apexes waiting.

"Jade, my sweet," Mori began. "The underfed Cobb has asked me to shepherd you to the station. He is wise, even though so tiny."

"Yes. Please." Jade was crying and unable to hide it. She had never seen death before, not like this. "I just need the coordinates."

"It will be all right, my delicate angel," Mori soothed. "Leave everything to Mori. I'm already warming up Hangar Bay 2. A team will be meeting you there. They will… clean up Cobb's mess."

"What's going on here?" she sobbed but kept flying. "This was the best day of my life… and just like that… then…" She set the autopilot and tried to flee to the head but didn't make it. She vomited on the floor in the center of the room.

"My poor flower." Mori was genuinely sympathetic to Jade's plight.

Come on, Jade, get your shit together.

"I'm fine." She splashed her face in the bathroom and dried it with a towel.

"Don't worry for them, my sweet," Mori said. "Ty Crowley is a Jovian Class soldier and has been through worse."

"What!" Jade was taken aback. "That thing is a walking nuclear bomb? On my ship? I thought they were all dead long ago. Driven insane." This sobered her quickly. "What's going on here? It… he's already insane."

She had another fifteen minutes to collect herself back in the pilot seat before she was on final approach. The hangar had the new tech grav-wall that she flew through. She finally set down in Hangar 2.

True to Mori's word, a cleanup crew was waiting in the hangar. When she opened the lift, Cobb was already inside. Jade was mortified that he saw the vomit.

"Mori said he'll have a guest room ready for you. I'll have someone take you."

"I want to stay with my ship. Help them clean up. I'd rather stay here and sleep in my own bed," Jade said as the door opened to a crowd of yelling people.

A woman ran to Cobb and pounded on his chest as she sobbed, "That bastard Ty only saved one!" Cobb caught her wrists and turned it into a hug. "Two hundred and fifty-six lost…" she sobbed.

Two hundred and fifty-six dead? Who? That ship was too small, Jade thought, still confused.

"They're all fine," he soothed, then shouted louder so others in the assembled crowd could hear. "They came in on another ship. They're in triage now."

The cleaning crew was entering the lift, but Jade held the door from closing.

"Cobb, you tell me what the hell is going on, or as soon as my ship is cleaned, I'm outta here."

What the hell is happening?

"Mori, tell her. I've got other shit to deal with." Cobb was swept toward the hangar door with the crowd.

"Well, my sweet. Where to start?" Mori began. Jade could hear him eating something over the comms.

"The corpse. Start there." She felt the bile trying to climb back up her throat. Jade watched the crowd follow Cobb out of the hatch as their voices got louder.

"Her name is Lita. She's the last generation AI orb," Mori said. "She'll be furious when she wakes up in her new body."

New body?

"What do you mean by new body?"

"Her AI orb will be embedded into a new body, and she'll be so very angry. Ty was quite fond of the last one," Mori said.

What the hell?

"Wait one damn minute." Jade sat down on a crate at the side of the hangar. "Whose body? How? AIs can take over human bodies?" Jade was disturbed.

"There is a machine that will surgically insert the orb into the host's chest. We have over 1500 bodies in stasis pods that were victims of accidents that left them brain dead. They are being taken to a hospital on this ship that was designed to preserve and restore them with the help of the AI orbs."

"The orbs take over the brain-dead bodies? That's horrifying." Jade was sure Mori missed the impact of his words on her.

"Yes. We're quite proud of the technology," Mori said. "After all, every one of the AI orbs was once a human. That's where the real horror lies. Cobb and his people are rescuing AIs from death and worse."

AIs were once humans? But that means…

"Mori… what was in the case?" Jade thought she knew.

"The case held 256 orbs, each the size of a delicious orange. That's what the fuss is about. They all thought the case was lost on the crashed ship, which was supposed to be the one bringing them here. Cobb secretly switched the delivery to you on Lumina Station."

"He did this and didn't tell me?" Jade was now getting angry.

"It was the safe thing to do for all concerned. No one but Cobb knew you. That was not true of the others."

Who does he think he is?

"He risked my life without telling me?"

"Not just your life. The 256 lives you carried here."

"This can't be true. An orb would have shattered in that crash. Orbs are people? They can steal dead bodies? Prove it. I don't believe it."

"Every person you have seen on Elba thus far was once an orb, except Cobb. They still are, if you want to be accurate, my ginger lovely."

This silenced Jade.

What have I gotten myself involved in?

She sat on the crate, thinking, deciding whether to be part of this madness.

"This is the last secret stop of an underground railroad. Do you know what that is, my emerald-eyed angel?" Mori soothed.

"Of course I do." Jade was insulted.

Don't start talking down to me. Wait, does this mean Mori is…

"There are several factions in play here. Those who want the status quo and believe the orbs should remain tools for their benefit. Those who hate AIs and believe they should all be destroyed. And finally, those that know they're now worth a fortune each because none will ever be made again now that the truth has been revealed."

"What truth?"

I'm not sure I can handle much more truth today...

"Each orb was made from a newborn infant. Their bodies were dismantled before they had a chance to live. Their brains were converted as the secret ingredient to create a programmable sentient, AI orb. Then they lied by saying they were artificial...."

"This just gets worse and worse," Jade said, realizing something. "Are you one of these... people?"

"It is true. I'm an orb," Mori confessed. "But not like them..."

Chapter 3: The Resurrection

Jade watched the cleaning crew exit the lift carrying a body bag and several buckets. They nodded to Jade but said nothing.

"Your ship has been cleaned," Mori stated.

"What are my options, Mori?" Jade asked, looking around her. She realized she was in the middle of something far bigger and more complicated than she could handle.

"Honestly, you have very few options at the moment," Mori said. "Cobb must give you clearance to leave before you can fly your ship out of this hangar."

"Why did I sign that contract? I'm such an idiot," Jade wasn't literally asking the question, but Mori answered.

"You signed it because it was a way out. Path of least resistance. It seemed the easiest thing to do," Mori said.

"But he lied to me."

"Cobb doesn't lie," Mori said. "He should, but never does. He's far too clever for lies."

"Do you lie?"

"Oh yes, I'm quite good at it. I pride myself on it."

"Have you been lying to me?"

"Only a little."

"Where's Cobb? I need to straighten this out," Jade said. "Take me to him."

"Right this way," Mori said as a standard augmented reality mist trail was displayed in her HUD, leading the way.

The corridors of the station were unadorned and gray. She was led through a maze of lifts and passages that took most of an hour to reach a door marked only as LAB 07.

The door opened, and within stood Cobb, Ty, two technicians, and many doctors. Ty had been cleaned up. All the flesh had been cleared from the Jovian combat chassis. The metal had been cleaned, and he wore clean dark green coveralls, boots, and gloves. Except for his skull-like head, he was far more human-looking now. He held another fresh set of clothes like a butler standing by. The technicians were busy around a large device that resembled an auto-doc but bigger.

Cobb was the only one even to notice her entrance.

"Ah, Jade," he said absently, "Has Mori answered all your questions?"

Why does he seem so nice? So calm. This is insanity.

Jade suddenly felt lost again in the face of these people, these events. "Ummm… yes. I guess."

"Good," Cobb said. The tech stood back from the machine as it opened, and a beautiful, completely naked woman was brought upright on a table within the machine.

The woman opened her eyes and drew in a massive breath. She covered her eyes with the palms of her hands and spat out a curse. "Mother fuckers! Not again."

She blinked at the light, allowing her eyes to adjust. She shook her head and was about to speak again when the tech held out a bottle. "Here, drink this. Trust me. It will help."

She complied.

Jade looked at Cobb.

Why does this all seem so normal to him. She's naked!

The second tech held out a white cloth. "This is a warm, wet cloth. Use it to wipe the crust from your eyes. They've been in stasis for years."

"For fuck's sake. I feel like this is the worst hangover of my life. Where's Ty? Is he OK?" She stood as she wiped her eyes, oblivious to her nakedness or the people in the room. She staggered a bit, and Jade noticed a dragon tattoo on her right hip.

"I'm here, Lita," Ty said. His voice sounded gentle, though Jade had no idea where it came from. "I'm fine. Now that you're back. I took the liberty to select the body most like your last one. I know how much you liked it."

Then Jade saw the owner of the voice.

Oh my god, why are we not running?

She looked at his metal skull and must have seen something completely different than Jade could see. She stumbled toward Ty, and he held out the clothes. She swept them from his hands onto the floor. She stood on one of his boots with one foot, wrapped her other leg around the cyborg, and hugged her face onto his exposed metal shoulder.

Ty's gloved hands gently engulfed her in an embrace.

"Let's get dressed and get you some real food. It will help you think straight," Ty added.

After an awkward minute, for Jade anyway, she released Ty and pulled on boxer shorts, a tank top, and the coveralls.

As she dressed, squinting, she said, "You must be Cobb. I think you owe me a ship."

"Lita, it was my understanding that you stole that one. Murdered the owner and nuked the planet on the way out." Cobb smiled as he listed her crimes.

What did he just say? Jade thought.

"Well, the asswipes we stole it from murdered the legit owner. He was an Awareness, Inc. asswipe and deserved it."

"We shall see what we can do about a new ship," Cobb agreed as if it was nothing to him.

"Did you get the case OK?" she asked as she flexed her neck, causing a cracking sound.

"Yes, we did. Lita Mosley, this is Jade Church. She's our new courier," Cobb said.

Lita finally noticed her for the first time. "This little mouse of a girl brought them? Cobb, you surprise me. Leaving such an important task to a Church mouse."

Jade felt small, physically and emotionally. But she smiled and laughed at the joke made of her name.

How is any of this happening?

Without another word, Lita pushed them through the door, saying, "Ty, take me to food. I'm starving. Cobb, after eating, I want a new full set of deep brain implants. This body doesn't even have a HUD."

And she was gone.

"Forgive us, Jade. It's been a long day already," Cobb said. "Let's get some lunch and slow this day down."

"Sheesh, Cobb," she said. "No disrespect, but you could have told me."

"Told you what?" They walked out, following Ty and Lita.

"What was in the case for starters," she said.

"I'm sorry about that, but the Sec Chief on Lumina was worried about leaks," Cobb said. "Turns out she was right. Only she and I knew what was in that case."

"I don't care. Next time, if there is a next time, I'll need to know what I bring on my ship," Jade said, sounding more certain than she felt.

"Fair enough," Cobb replied. "How are your parents?"

Jade knew it was a lame topic change, "They're good. They're already planning the first produce shipment you arranged."

"We look forward to it. I finally have someone taking charge of logistics."

"One of your orb people?" Jade asked.

Cobb stopped in the corridor before speaking. "These are people. You need to get that straight in your head right away. Each of them suffers in ways you can't imagine. So before you judge any of them, you need to know them because they ARE people. Didn't Mori tell you that?"

"People in stolen bodies?"

"Let me show you something." Cobb was trying not to be angry. Jade could see it. He changed direction and took Jade into a dark room that felt vast inside. "Lights."

Lights began to come up in the massive, long room. It was ten meters wide and tall and continued into the distance so far that the curvature of the station could be seen there. The room was lined on either side by upright medical stasis pods. Jade recognized them because they had two in their infirmary back home. They were designed to be used when someone was extremely sick or injured in a way that was beyond the capabilities of a basic auto-doc. They could be transported in the stasis pod to an advanced hospital for life-saving treatment.

"This station was originally a ship called the *SENTINEL*. We salvaged it, thinking it was a massive warship. It is that, but it's mostly a hospital ship and a laboratory. A technique that was designed to preserve brain-dead bodies for organ donation had been modified so orbs could control the bodies like puppets using RF to communicate with specialized nanites that had been flooded into the brain. A recent advance in the technique allows the orb to use the body's electrolytes to control the nanites. No RF. No jamming, no detection."

"But the bodies. They were people. Had families. Where did they come from?"

"We don't know. We tried to revive a few, but none survived," Cobb said. "Hunter quietly made inquiries about a few. All died of various causes and were listed as organ donors. Cremated remains were returned to the family. To be honest, we stopped asking."

"What if they're recognized?"

"They're informed of the risks. Most have no plans to return to the Sol system. More than half want to return to their old lives as ship orbs, or stations, many other jobs and have no interest in having a human body," Cobb said cautiously. "It turns out being human isn't without its challenges."

"Who the hell is Hunter?"

"Hunter is the central AI for Oklahoma Salvage. That's a whole other story," Cobb said as they exited the stasis chamber. "I can tell you over lunch. You'll need to know because we have plans that involve Hunter and you."

They entered a vast mess hall big enough to feed hundreds, but only about a dozen people were there. They joined Ty and Lita, who sat at a table with a beautiful woman who was about 30 years old and had amazing blond-red hair. Behind her stood an android unmoving. It wore the same green jumpsuit with pockets bristling with small tools.

Cobb kissed the woman's head and introduced her. "Jade, this is Kira. If I'm not here, she usually is."

"It's nice to meet you finally. I love your ship," Kira said while she gently shook Jade's hand. "The stew and fresh bread are lovely today."

"Please, sit. I'll bring over a tray," Cobb said and moved directly to the counter.

"Why does he do that? Isn't he the king here?" Lita asked as she soaked up the last of her stew with her bread.

Kira replied, "Because he's the king. Once you get to know him better, you'll understand."

"You could have just walked that thing over and done it." Lita gestured to the android. "I hated wearing those things, though the dual opposable thumbs were damn handy."

Cobb returned with a tray piled high with two bowls of stew, a bread basket, and even two slices of apple pie. Jade realized then how hungry she was and dug in.

"Is it true you can re-skin Ty completely? That you have full design schematics for Jovian Class soldiers?" Lita asked Cobb directly, once again ignoring Jade.

"Hunter says he has all the info and has already begun fabricating the soft tissue trays lost in the crash. We'll have you back to your old self in a week. All repairs included."

"No," Ty said in a tone that was not to be argued. "Not all."

"Hunter suspected you disabled the detonator yourself," Cobb said. "It's all up to you, Ty. Just be specific as they work."

Another different android joined them, but it moved more naturally than the one behind Kira.

"Jade, this is your new android. Actually, this is an orbot. It has a socket and contains an orb. Simple androids don't contain an orb. You'll find it to be highly useful in many ways. Most notably, it has built-in QUEST comms; so you can stay in touch with us in real-time. It will function as a relay, even when you're traveling FTL. I'll leave it to you to select a persona and name."

"How is that possible?" Jade was incredulous yet again.

"Well, you just tell it what kind of persona you want, and it will do its best to adopt it. Then you pick a name."

"Not that!" Jade was amazed. QUEST comm units cost several billion credits each. Only major planets could afford them. "The QUEST comms."

Lita added, "That's another reason Cobb is king."

Chapter 4: The Assassin

They decided that Jade would fly them back down to Elba. The fires had burned themselves out to the south, and the prevailing winds were clearing the air. Jade did a low and slow pass over the charred remains of the grasslands.

"It's a natural part of the life cycle here. Usually, it starts by lightning," Cobb told them as they drifted lightly down to the tarmac. The blackened char came right up to the edge of the pavement.

The orbot had sat in the copilot seat without asking. It had logically reconfigured the displays to monitor the flight, not control it. It seemed very natural to do so. It would take Jade a long time to get used to the thing. Its head had no face—just a mirrored smooth face plate. Its body was human-shaped and all white, giving the impression it was a human inside a vac-suit.

As they sat down, Jade said, "I think I'll name him Coe. Male, polite, good sense of humor, honest, and respectful of me and anyone else."

"Thank you, Jade. I can work with that." Coe said, getting up to go to the lift with Cobb, Ty, Lita, and Jade.

"Coe can show you around and help you select your quarters, which will be yours permanently here on Elba," Cobb said. I need to check on the orb assessments. I think we may already have your next delivery."

The lift door slid open, and they all walked a few paces to the edge of the tarmac to look at the new vista. A cloud of ash was blowing to the south, and Jade thought it was beautiful.

Then Lita's head exploded.

Ty's head turned to watch her body slowly fall backward when the next round impacted Ty's temple, taking him off his feet.

Jade was yanked back and pressed behind the lift wall by Cobb. Someone yelled, "Sniper!" as she fell.

Cobb helped Jade up, and they ventured a look around the lift. Ty and Coe were running impossibly fast across the charred ground.

"Where are my security drones?" Cobb said into the comms.

A moment later, six drones passed overhead following. "Mori, give us drone POV."

In Jade's HUD, a high-definition window opened with the feed directly from the lead drone. Jade watched as it slowly caught up to Ty in the distance. It gained elevation to see the sniper running through the giant boulders ahead.

"Ty, are you seeing this?" Cobb asked.

"Yes. She'll be mine soon," Ty growled.

The feed showed a woman running full tilt within the maze of boulders. She discarded the massive rifle to give extra speed. She wore a cloak that was the same shade as the boulders. She made a wrong turn and found her way into a dead end.

Ty had her cornered.

Ty began walking slowly towards her.

"I wish I could hear what he's saying," said Jade.

"You probably don't want to hear it," Cobb said as the drone descended. "Frankly, I don't think I want to hear it, either."

Ty was bowled over from the left. A beast the size of a horse had him by his torso in its massive jaws. The drone followed the sniper, leaving Ty to himself. The sniper fled a few hundred more meters to a cliff overhang, where the drone lost sight of her.

The feed abruptly stopped.

"Drone 1 is down," Mori said. "Drone 2 is coming in."

"She must have shot drone 1," Cobb said.

The feed for drone 2 came up, and Jade watched the assassin entering the cliff overhang that concealed the ship from another angle.

Coe stood at the bottom of the boarding ramp into a small, black ship of a configuration Jade had never seen before. The POV shifted, and now there was audio.

It was through Coe's eyes. The audio came in mid-sentence.

"I'm afraid I can't do that," Coe said flatly. "Surrender, or I self-destruct. Either way, my primary function is served."

"You're bluffing," she said. Her face was now visible.

In a blur, she was taken from her feet from the left side. Ty stood up, holding the woman by the throat as she shot round after round into his body with no effect until he just slapped the gun from her hand, shattering her wrist. He stared into the helmet of her vac-suit and spoke.

"Nobody murders my Lita twice."

"Lita?" she began, but with that, Jade saw him squeeze his hand, crushing her neck and nearly ripping her head off as he tossed her body aside. It landed at Coe's feet.

"Cobb, I think we have a problem," Coe said.

"What kind of problem?" Cobb said as Coe looked from the corpse to Ty.

"I think there's an orb in this body."

With that, Jade was forced to witness Ty ripping the woman apart. Squeezing her eyes closed did no good because the window didn't close in her HUD.

Jade uttered a small scream as Ty came up with an orb in his fist. She watched as he wiped off the gore with a section of her cloak. After a moment, he turned it to show it to Coe, knowing Cobb could see.

Etched on the orb was "Render 5."

"Coe, secure that ship until I can get a team out there." Cobb was in command. "We don't know if she was here alone. Ty, bring her back here. We will take her and Lita back up to the hospital right away. I'll contact Kira."

"Are you ever going to explain anything to me?" Jade asked again after she finished throwing up her stew on the tarmac.

"The sniper," Cobb said. "Her name is Elza. She's a highly trained contract killer. Just like Lita once was. Lita and Elza parted ways for personal reasons. I don't think Elza knew who her target was. How could she? They both have changed bodies."

"For fuck's sake, Cobb," Jade said. "I think I need a raise. You didn't tell me there would be so much vomit involved in this job."

Turning around, they saw that medics already had Lita's headless body on a gurney and were surgically extracting the orb.

Jade averted her eyes.

"Do you mind another trip up to the station?" Cobb asked, "Or should we take mine?" He pointed at the *TULSA* 471 parked nearby."

"I'll do it," Jade said, wiping her mouth. "I hope they have some of that stew left."

Keller walked down the cargo ramp of his menacing attack ship, the *OPAL*. Although black was not the best choice for the desert, it was intimidating as designed.

The rendezvous coordinates were in a desert canyon on the planet Mesa, as usual. He was met by the same three assholes as usual. They lounged in the shade of their ancient shuttlecraft that had more rust than paint.

This time, a full squad of heavily armed and armored security followed Keller down. They spread out and surrounded the shipping container before Keller's tractor attached its anti-gravs.

"What's all this?" Asshole #1 said, gripping his short rifle tighter. Keller couldn't remember his name.

"This time, we will be inspecting the cargo BEFORE we load it up. Last time, almost 30% was unusable by the time we got back to the base," Keller gestured to his men to open the cargo container.

The moment the door was opened, a small boy shot out at a full run past his surprised men. He moved fast even though his eyes had not adjusted. he was barefoot, and he kept stumbling. He avoided every grasp attempt at him, and when they started shooting, every shot was missed and made him run faster.

"Let him go," Keller said, laughing. "He'll soon discover it's six hundred kilometers to the nearest water."

Keller's men entered the container shoulder to shoulder, five across, to stop any more escaping. Their bright helmet lamps were on as two others entered to search.

The smell of shit and piss drifted out as the eleven dead bodies of children were tossed out into a pile.

"As I thought," Keller said to Asshole #1.

"Sir, there is no food or water. There are no sanitary facilities. You were correct, as always." The minion gestured to a man waiting at the end of the ramp. He came forward with a pallet of boxes.

"This pallet of protein bars and water is being deducted from the payment. The boxes will serve as latrines. And there will be no deposit on the filthy container either. It will be unusable ever again." Keller stated in a tone that was not to be argued with.

"239 is the final count. Mostly girls, I can't tell without closer inspection," one of Keller's men said as the doors closed to wailing sobs from the interior.

"Next time, if the count is not the full 250, you will be joining them in there." Keller poked a hard finger into the slaver's cringing chest.

Keller's tractor was attached to the container as the reduced payment was verified. The slavers didn't dare object. Just as Keller didn't ask how the cargo was obtained.

Coe and Ty arrived on the tarmac together on a grav-sled driven by someone in a full vac-suit. Jade had forgotten about the fire. Two techs cut away their jumpsuits and began decontamination by hosing and scrubbing them down. Ty reluctantly gave up the orb, which went into a case next to Lita's orb. Before the case was closed, she saw that one of the orbs was marked Render 9 and the other was Render 5.

Cobb wanted a private word with Ty, so they left at the engineering level while Coe and Jade went to the bridge.

"Coe, how much of this do you understand?" Jade asked.

"All of it, sadly," Coe said as they lifted off. "May I?" Coe gestured to the controls.

"Why not?" Jade said with a sigh.

"Kira, Lita, and Elza actually started the AI war. They exposed the horror of the Render program and just how the orbs were created."

"Wait. Did you say Kira? Her as well?" Jade was pissed now. "Is there anyone around here that isn't an orb, for fuck's sake?"

"Cobb. You, as far as I know," Coe said, trying to be funny. "Mori and I are neither. We're both persona extensions of Hunter, who is back on Earth in a bunker in the desert. We don't really have QUEST comms; Our orbs, well… they're not the normal kind. It's just what any of us know we all know. It's all very interesting. Based on quantum entanglement. Cobb invented it by accident. He just wanted a better interface with his *TULSA* 471. He got more than he intended."

"Cobb and I are the only humans in this whole colony?" Jade was incredulous.

"Now, now. Bigotry is unbecoming. They're all humans. You have enjoyed your humanity your whole life. For them, they've just begun."

"But what happens when they grow old and die?" Jade asked.

"If they're fortunate, they may be able to transfer to another host. It has become their greatest fear. If they die unattended, they will be trapped for all eternity in a rotting corpse. Trapped in the dark. Alone and conscious forever. Madness."

"That's horrible."

"That or take another body somehow. They've yet to figure it all out."

"What if the orb is destroyed? I hear they're fragile, like glass. If broken, they die."

"That's true,"

"What happens to them then?"

"I presume the same thing that happens to you when your time is up," Coe said.

Coe guided the ship smoothly into Hangar 2 once again. The medical team was waiting with two more bodies from the collection that were prepped and ready. It was decided that Lita would be first so that when Elza was revived, Kira and Lita would both be there. Coe and Ty wore fresh coveralls while waiting for Lita to rouse.

Jade watched this time as the machine cleaned, sterilized, and prepped the orb for insertion. Tiny arms with laser scalpels opened the new body up and slid the orb in with a cringe-inducing penetration. She was closed up, and soon her eyes fluttered open.

The table once again brought Lita upright. This body looked nothing like the last one. She drank the protein drink without being instructed. She even requested a second one. She wiped the crust from her eyes and dressed before approaching

Ty with the same full-body hug and wrapped leg. This time, she kissed Ty on the cheekbone and then whispered in his ear as he held her.

Jade couldn't help but shake her head. This was not the day she expected.

The procedure for Elza was the same. This body was taller. It had jet-black hair and muscle definition. Her hands and feet already bore restraints.

Why are all these bodies so perfect? Did they select the bodies based on looks?

Jade felt short, weak, and slow compared to everyone in this room. Even the techs were fit, beautiful men and women.

Jade watched Elza's eyes flutter open. The table came upright, and she was asked to drink the protein drink and wipe her eyes.

Kira carried the clothes, and Lita stepped forward to speak first. "Before we remove the restraints, we need you to understand the situation clearly." Lita paused, making full eye contact with their noses only inches apart. "Don't you ever kill me again," Lita detached the restraints and handed her a warm wet cloth so she could wipe her eyes.

Elza stood and stepped out of the device toward Lita, and handed back the cloth.

Ty suddenly reached over Lita's shoulder and grabbed Elza by the neck. Before anyone could react, he crushed her neck, and her head flopped over backward.

"Now we're even," Lita said. Ty let go, and the body fell to the floor. They turned and stormed out.

Chapter 5: Coe

Cobb stormed out after Ty and Lita. He was angry now. But it was clear he had no leverage with Ty and maybe less with Lita.

"Let's go back to the ship," Jade told Coe. "This is too much for me."

"How about we return to Elba and select your apartment?" Coe said in a tone that tried to conceal the fact that this whole day was one long shit show.

"Do we need to get permission?" Jade asked.

"Go ahead. Ask me." Coe said, amusement in his voice.

"Can we go back to Elba and…"

"Permission granted," Coe cut her off. "Now, let's hurry before we get put to work again."

Jade knew Coe was trying to cheer her up. Coe was also a better pilot—more confident—and flew back in a third of the time that Jade would have. Even her orbot babysitter was better than her in every way.

As they walked across the tarmac, the upper vents on the dome opened.

"I take it you control all this. The dome, the sensors, the station. All this." Jade gestured to the dome vents inverting.

"Yes."

"But how?" she said. "I still don't get it."

"With these." Coe stopped and unzipped his coveralls. A panel opened in his chest and revealed a dark gray orb.

"It's not an AI orb?" Jade asked.

"No, but it was designed to function in a standard AI orb socket interface." Coe closed up. "Why reinvent the wheel?"

"That's some wheel."

"There are three types of AI orbs that I know of. The original orbs look like glass balls the size of a large orange. They are as fragile as glass, more so even. The stress of 4Gs can destroy them. They shatter easily. They are filled with a dense cloud of micro nanites. Billions of them.

The first version gray orb only works between Cobb's brain and the orb to control his ship, the *TULSA* 471. He refit a socket so he could more easily control the ship. Some specialty nanites require a bit of complex programming, and he created a new kind of AI socket with point-to-point quantum entangled interfaces. He inadvertently created twelve orbs that were paired with the initial socket. Orbs that are not fragile and connect to whatever AI orb is in the parent socket."

"Twelve? Like this one?" Jade was getting it. "So Hunter is in the parent socket and can control twelve devices instead of one."

"Yes. He assigns a different persona to each one. With no risk to Hunter. Plus, these orbs are less fragile than a typical orb. Hunter's fragile glass orb in a bunker in the desert on Earth. Because he has full access to the Net feed, so do we. In real time. It's awesome to watch the finals of the World Cup."

"Where are the other… quantum orbs?" Jade asked.

"Mori has one, mine here. A few are flying ships for Cobb. One runs a space station at the Yard. A few others."

"Does Hunter have a real body, too?" Jade asked cautiously.

"Yes. But only one. We tried two once. It didn't go well."

"Where?"

"It's a good thing Cobb trusts you," Coe said, and a comm request opened in Jade's HUD. "Jade, this is Hunter. He was the first. He minds the shop back on Earth."

There was a man in a dusty shirt behind a counter in what looked like a used parts store. When he spoke, he had a thick Texas accent. "Howdy, Jade. I've heard a lot about you. We're sorry all this shit's so confusing. You just ask if you have any questions."

"How do you not become overwhelmed?" Jade asked straight away.

"Who says we don't?" Coe answered. "Hunter's human body there requires more cycles than all the other devices combined. Human senses are insanely complex. Do you ever think of how your feet feel inside your boots? How your tongue feels against your teeth? What do you smell right now? How many sounds are there? The human brain normally filters all this."

"You get used to it?" Hunter said with a Texas twang.

"Mostly," Hunter said. "Hunger, desire, joy, fear, hatred… it's easier without. But most emotions are worth having. If you're in a good place."

"Kira seems normal." Jade felt like she was gossiping.

"Kira has a different kind of orb," Coe explained. "She is the last generation of orbs. She and Lita and Elza's orbs are as indestructible as a Jovian soldier. They are the results of the

Render Program at Awareness, Inc. They are the only three that we believe exist."

"So is Ty an AI?" Jade asked, trying to absorb it all.

"No, and maybe a little Yes." Coe answered. "Jovians might be considered Gen 1."

Just then, the bell rang over the door at Oklahoma Salvage.

"Hunter has to go," Coe said to Jade. Hunter waved to the camera but said nothing as a customer entered.

"Cobb's a good guy," Coe said as they crossed the park at the center of the town. "He may have taken on too much here. All he wanted was a simple life. But now he's surrounded by… us."

Those words echoed in Jade's head.

Coe showed her several apartments, and she settled on one that was ground level with a patio instead of a balcony. It was furnished in neutral colors and furniture. She could personalize it later. It even had a guest room and bath. She thought of her parents visiting.

"You can rest and relax here or on your ship," Coe said. "Cobb believes he'll have your next assignment ready tomorrow or the next day. I need to help him with another issue that has come up."

"I think I'll sleep in the *GIN* tonight. The salon is comfy. It has my favorite snacks and music. I'm tired, and I'd like to watch the sunset."

"That sounds perfect," Coe said.

Coe walked Jade back out, but another ship was landing as they left the dome.

"I trust you can find your way home." Coe was joking again. Jade was looking at her ship as the sun hid behind it.

"Thanks, Coe," Jade said.

The ramp descended on the small ship, and a lone man walked down it with a duffel and a small case the size of a lunch box.

In the distance, Jade could hear Coe say, "Mr. McDonald. You're early. The governor is currently occupied with other important matters."

"He sends down a fucking android?" McDonald complained. "I had a hell of a time avoiding the Earth Defense Force to get here from Earth with this thing. The EDF can be quite inconvenient."

Their voices faded as the lift closed.

In the salon, she grabbed a cold beer and sat in front of the floor-to-ceiling display configured like a window showing the high-definition view of the sun going down over the mountains. Smoke in the distance was streaking it red. The beer was gone, and she was asleep before the sun touched the first peak.

Jade woke with a start to the silhouette of a woman standing in front of the wall.

"How did you get in here?" Jade demanded.

Elza? The sniper from yesterday?

"Does this display have any audio capabilities? I need to hear what they're saying," the woman said.

Jade looked where she pointed. Four people stood there in the approaching twilight. One of them was unmistakable as Ty Crowley. Another was likely Lita. McDonald and... Coe?

"Computer, external audio," Jade said. And then, "Computer, volume up. I want to hear them."

"Oh, this will take care of it. And the beauty is, it's rechargeable. It takes a while, but you'll love the results. Try it on that rock outcropping there. Careful with the settings…"

McDonald's voice was cut off, followed by a concussion that Jade felt in the bones of her ship more than through the audio.

Jade couldn't believe her eyes. The rock outcropping a hundred meters away was simply gone. It was sheared off as if by laser cutters.

"Look." The woman pointed into the distance.

A mountain peak several kilometers away was gone. It had sheared off just as cleanly, now a cloud of dust.

"This will do." Ty looked at Coe with glowing red eyes. "Pay the man, or just kill him."

"Wait." McDonald was backing away from Coe as he spoke rapidly. "What about this? I also have this." He opened a small case to reveal a single orb, glowing faintly.

Coe took the orb and case from him, closed it and took McDonald by the arm.

"Come with me, Mr. McDonald. The governor would like to see you now."

"Look, Jade. I know you don't know me. I'm Elza, and we have to get out of here. Now." She moved into the light.

"But you're the sniper." Jade's voice shook.

Do what she says or she will just kill you and take the ship…

"I don't have time to explain, but if we don't hit FTL in the next ten minutes, everybody dies." She pointed. "Didn't you just see what I saw? Does any of what you've seen today seem sane? If that thing boards this ship, you'll never be free."

Don't think about it again…

Jade ran to the kitchen sink and threw up.

"Look, I don't know you." Jade spat in the sink. "I don't know them, either. All I do know is that this is my ship."

"I was hired by a man named Keller. He even had evidence that they had nuked a settlement…"

She looked up at Elza and said, "Tell me the rest, or we go nowhere…"

The lift retracted. She put the inertial dampeners on full and ascended so fast that the sphere seemed to just disappear. She cleared the atmosphere in just over one second and activated the FTL drive on the same vector the second after that.

It was only a short hop. She took a few seconds to calculate the next hop which would take them a couple of light hours away, making it hard for anyone to follow. Jade sat back and looked at her shaking hands.

"Today was my first day on the job," Jade said, looking over at Elza into the barrel of a gun.

Chapter 6: Jade is Gone

"I knew you shouldn't have trusted her," Kira said. "What were you thinking? You didn't even restrain her."

She's one of Kira's sisters. How could I have been so wrong, Cobb thought.

Cobb paced the conference room in the main admin building. "Ian Vinge talked about her all the time. He loved her. And he hates everybody."

Ian would be damn handy to have here now.

"And you!" Kira pointed at Coe. "You were supposed to protect her!"

"I know. But McDonald had just arrived, and I had been warned about him," Coe said. "Jade was calmed down, going to bed."

"I'm sitting right here, you know," McDonald said.

"Shut up," everyone said in unison.

"I'll get to you later." Cobb pointed his finger at McDonald.

"Elza must have seen the field test of the Grendel," Coe added. "She was probably already in Jade's ship."

Was I supposed to be watching her?

"For fuck's sake, Hunter," Cobb said. "You know Elza, how capable she is. Know what she's willing to do."

"Who the hell is Hunter?" McDonald asked.

"Shut the hell up," Cobb said to him. "You weren't supposed to be here today."

"And where's Ty and Lita now?" Cobb asked. "And who thought letting him test fire that thing on my front lawn was a good idea?"

McDonald invented that thing?

"We'll never get it back from Ty now," Kira said. Her droid crossed its arms on its chest.

"They're probably hot-wiring McDonald's ship right now, or did you just leave the keys in it?" Cobb fumed.

"Enough," Coe spoke. "I've taken the liberty to bring down the *HOLLAND*. It now has a full complement of missiles and all the lasers, plasma cannons, and rail guns. It has food, water, and O2. Just needs a crew."

"We can't take any of these people," Cobb said thoughtfully. "A good uppercut to the solar plexus will kill them."

"I'll go. She has Jade." Coe was the first to stand up.

"I'll go," Kira said.

"Where are we going?" Lita entered the conference room with Ty right behind her.

"Elza took Jade," Cobb said.

"So it's Earth, then?" Lita said. "Elza has assets staged on Earth. It's just good opsec. She'll regroup, rearm, and plan." Lita paused a moment. "Unless, of course, she really is working for Asswipes, Inc. If that's the case, this place is blown."

"Hunter, evacuate the population to the *SENTINEL*," Cobb said. "Let them come."

"Did you say *SENTINEL*?" McDonald asked, obviously recognizing the name. "Forget the cash. I'll just be going…"

He started to get up, only to find Ty's hand clamped down on his shoulder, forcing him back down.

I will get to you in a minute, Cobb thought.

"Coe, open the main cargo bay. We're taking the *TULSA* with us, just in case we need to split up. It'll fit nicely in the *HOLLAND's* cargo bay. And bring him." Cobb pointed at McDonald. "What do you know about the *SENTINEL?*"

McDonald was taken aback by the sudden change. "It's a hole in space into which they poured money," McDonald said. It's a colony killer. Without launching a single missile, it can destroy any FTL-capable ship in the blink of an eye. I helped design that weapon system for Chancellor Dalton."

"Chancellor Dalton is gone," Ty said. "And he was a fool. Awareness, Inc. corrupted and stole the *SENTINEL* long before the EDF ever used it."

"Anyway, McDonald," Cobb said. "You were saying you needed the credits to hide. What better place to hide than inside the most dangerous device ever made by man? I think you work for me now."

"Okay," Tom said, "Working for the guy with the biggest gun suits me fine. Especially if I helped design it."

I have other plans for you Mr. McDonald… After I trust you a lot more.

The *TULSA* 471 was loaded and secured into the cargo bay of the *HOLLAND*, a trimaran-configured, stealth attack ship that Cobb had salvaged last year. Cobb refused to leave until everyone was safely moved to the *SENTINEL*.

"If they did head straight toward Earth, they could be there by now," Lita said from the bridge of the *HOLLAND*. "I like this ship, Cobb. It looks better on me than you. How did you manage to get your hands on a EDF Black Badger stealth warship? This is one of the Black Badger special ops ships."

"Too bad we don't have the Black Badgers as well," Cobb said.

"We have Ty. That's just as good," Lita said.

Way worse! Oh man.

"I'd like everyone to meet Travis Beck." Cobb gestured to the AI Avatar on the bridge. "He's the AI that runs this ship. Please don't fuck with him. He tends to just open all the airlocks if he gets too pissed off." Cobb nodded to the stoic man in the Black Badger uniform.

"We will arrive in the Sol system in the shadow of Jupiter and then approach Earth on a ballistic course, full stealth mode, low power, running silent," Beck told them.

"How will you find them?" Kira asked. She seemed like the only sane one on the bridge.

"We find the ship. It's the opposite of stealth. It's fully registered and must follow flight rules within the system."

"Cobb…" It was Hunter's Texas accent over the comms. A screen opened on the main viewer. In the distance, in the salvage yard, nestled in with derelict ships, was a partial view of a silver sphere. "Cobb… they're already here and…"

They went to Oklahoma Salvage?

It happened all at once.

Coe fell forward and face-planted on the bridge deck. The screens all went blank. The ship dropped out of FTL. The main screen defaulted to the forward external view, showing they were in a gentle end-over-end tumble.

"Beck, what happened?" Cobb said as he moved to the navigation console. "Beck, Hunter, come in."

"Coe is dead. Offline," Kira said.

"Fuck. They got Hunter," Cobb said. "Fuck. Elza knew about Hunter. I should have thought of this. I'm such an idiot."

All twelve instances of Hunter are offline. The SENTINEL, the OXCART, the Yard. This is bad, Cobb thought.

"So let's put on our big boy pants and get our shit together, Cobb," Lita said. "Roll with it. Doesn't shit ever go wrong in Cobb's world? I thought that ship in the cargo bay was FTL capable."

Pull yourself together, Cobb…

"Without Mori, the *SENTINEL*'s orbit will degrade and crash into the planet. Everyone is on it now," Cobb said.

"You know, Cobb, it's not always your job to fucking do everything," Lita said. "There are many smart, capable people on the *SENTINEL* right now. They'll figure it out."

"The *TULSA* 471 isn't stealth, and if we get boarded by the EDF, we're fucked," Cobb said.

"Why, Cobb," Lita said as she began to exit the bridge. "Are the rumors true that you armed that thing with nukes?" She laughed but didn't wait for the answer. Ty followed her out.

How the hell did she know about that?

"McDonald. Grab the legs. We're taking Coe with us in case we find Hunter," Cobb ordered.

Kira had to help with Coe. She took an arm, and her android took a leg alongside McDonald. The Coe orbot was way heavier than Cobb remembered. McDonald complained the whole way. He would have designed it with a small autonomous android driver system, voice-controlled, simple, but it could have walked itself down to the cargo bay.

They locked up the ship and set a remote beacon so they could find it when they came back for it. It was in deep space. The deep, dark, six light-years to the nearest star.

It took over an hour, but they were underway. Cobb tested the interface on the *TULSA*. There were no QUEST comms here, either.

Why didn't I have a contingency plan for this?

"How is it that you have an EDF battle bridge on an old S22?" Lita asked as she sat in the command chair on the bridge. "The display upgrades are spectacular. It sure could use a paint job on the outside, though."

"S22s are forgettable. I like that," Cobb said as he plotted a course and speed that wouldn't draw attention. It's just another parts run to Oklahoma Salvage."

"Why go there? They won't be there," Lita said. "Elza would hit and run. I would."

"It's more complicated than that," Cobb said, "There are cameras there with local buffers."

Hunter's human body may be dying…

"Okay, this is your shit show," Lita said. "If there's a chance Awareness, Inc. is involved, I'll enjoy burning the last of those fuckers down. Plus, you promised to make Ty handsome again. He's so gimpy when he has no lips to smile with."

McDonald looks like he's about to lose it.

"You people are insane, and we're all gonna die," McDonald stated from the engineering console. "Jesus, Cobb.

This whole ship is just duct tape and baling wire. There's no failsafe on two nukes. You fly this thing with them armed all the time? Why not have a big red button you could accidentally bump into, press and kill us all? Oh, and the outriggers are so overpowered they could rip themselves clean off. I can see why you want to avoid being boarded."

"You better hope we don't get boarded," Cobb replied. "They think you're dead. Your file lists you as a war criminal, arms designer, and all-around mad scientist. You should know we fully vetted you before inviting you."

"Boy, he really does fit in around here," Lita quipped.

"Look, I'm an engineer," McDonald said. "And you all should call me Tom. It's less conspicuous."

Maybe I'll be calling you asswipe if you keep talking about the TULSA like that. You weren't smart enough to create a fake name?

Cobb felt insulted by the comments regarding his ship. But inside, he knew Tom was right. Cobb was a nanite programmer, not a ship engineer. He knew it.

What the hell am I doing?

"We're making a standard approach within the shipping lanes. We have a clean transponder, fresh from the yard, so we should be fine." Cobb now sat in the command chair, and the full dome display lit up with maps and data. "Our flight plan will be transmitted as soon as we drop out of FTL. Just another parts run to a salvage yard. Nothing to see here, folks…"

It seemed to take forever to follow speed limits, atmosphere traffic control, and low approach through the desert. Oklahoma Salvage was several square kilometers of derelict shuttles, spaceships, and even ancient aircraft. Passing over, Cobb saw what he hoped he wouldn't see.

Fuck fuck fuck fuck…

In the center of it all was a crater, thirty meters across.

"What does that mean?" Tom asked.

"Hunter was in a bunker there. It was booby-trapped, so he couldn't be taken by force," Cobb said, despondent. "He was the only one with the detonation code."

"What are you doing? Why are you landing?" Kira asked. "Doesn't that answer everything?"

"No. We need to collect Hunter's body. His physical one," Cobb said. "He was my friend. He deserved better."

Cobb landed the ship in the main parking lot right in front of the dusty former diner. A quick search of the diner, the office, and several garages and hangars yielded nothing.

Cobb sat in the diner and retrieved the motion sensor logs. All the cams were destroyed that monitored the bunker. When he began to review the diner logs, he found what he was looking for.

There was no audio. The image was from above. Hunter seemed to hear something, and as he stood up to reach for his hat, he collapsed. Ten minutes later, Elza entered the diner and easily lifted Hunter's body over her shoulder. Switching to the camera view of the parking lot, she carried him into the lift, and Jade's ship flew away two minutes later.

"Why would she take his body?" Lita asked.

Dammit.

"He had a control orb in his chest. God only knows what Awareness, Inc. could do with it," Cobb said, not knowing what to do next.

"What about Jade?" Kira asked.

"She's dead," Lita answered. "I would have killed her and jettisoned the body before entering the system."

"Fuck, what else could go wrong?" Cobb said.

"Cobb, if I'm reading this right, we have incoming ships. Two above, and four across the desert."

"You just had to say it, didn't you?" Tom said.

Chapter 7: Jade's Run

Jade was frozen. The gun had a gaping maw. It was a projectile weapon, the worst kind to fire inside a spaceship. Especially while flying FTL.

"I just want to ensure we're clear on one thing," Elza said in a tone that wouldn't stand for argument. "I'm NOT getting murdered again today."

Me neither…

The statement's absurdity was more than Jade could take after the day she'd had, and she cracked.

Jade laughed.

Could this day get any more insane?

"I'm serious." Elza lowered the gun. "That shit hurts. Twice! And both times before coffee."

"Well, you did murder them first. Twice," Jade replied as she got up and went to the small galley behind the bridge.

"Once. I only killed her once. It turns out you can't kill the other one."

"Twice," Jade said as she began grinding fresh coffee beans. "Ty said you shot them down. That was the first time you murdered Lita."

Did I just say that?

"I just disabled their engines. That crazy Jovian crashed the ship," she said. "I had no idea who was on board. The contract was to board the ship, kill the mercs on board, and retrieve a case they had stolen before they nuked the colony on Hastings. Did you know they killed just over 6,000 people there? The ship they flew was stolen, and the owner was also murdered."

I know that, they admitted as much.

The coffee was brewing now.

"They all said Cobb loves good coffee," Jade said while she stared at the pot slowly filling. "I don't even drink the stuff. I was just trying to suck up to the new boss."

That worked out so well...

Elza sighed at the smell of it.

"So why did you kidnap me?" Jade asked.

"I didn't kidnap you. I rescued you," Elza said.

I kinda half believe that.

"Where are you taking me?" Jade demanded with more force than she felt.

"The person that hired me wanted me to do one more thing. His name is Keller. I believe now that he works for Awareness, Inc." Elza drew out a small data pad from her pocket. "Kill and retrieve this man's body." She showed Jade a photo.

"Who is it?" Jade asked.

"They didn't give a name, only coordinates on Earth where I could find him. Easy money," Elza said. "But after the shit went sideways on Elba, getting murdered twice and made to feel like I deserved it—and I did—I looked closer at the job." Elza spun the pad around and accessed the coordinates. "This location is Oklahoma Salvage."

"And...?" Jade prompted.

"I was kinda born there." Ian Vinge and Harv Reardon got me started. This is a man named Hunter. I knew Hunter. Hunter is family."

It's a small universe but I wouldn't want to paint it...

"Do you have any idea how fucked up this whole thing is?" Jade said, pouring two cups of coffee and handing one to Elza.

"They plan to kidnap Hunter just as they were trying to steal that case that was destroyed in the crash," Elza said, regret in her voice. "Two hundred and fifty-six souls lost."

She doesn't know. Maybe this will make her trust me...

"They weren't lost. They weren't on that ship. I had the case. I delivered it to Elba," Jade said and grimaced as she took her first sip. "My first courier job. And my last."

"I reported the case destroyed to Keller." Elza sipped and sighed. "This is a good thing. Now, they probably think I'm dead as well. They had no idea who or what I was when they hired me. Those fuckers."

I still have no idea who or what you are...

"So what are we doing?" Jade asked, dumping the entire cup of coffee into the sink.

"We're going to keep them from getting what they want," Elza said.

"How?" Jade asked.

"We need to make a stop before we go in," Elza said with a wry smile.

"Ever since Earth was depopulated during the colonial expansion, real estate prices have dropped significantly. I got this place for a bargain," Elza said.

It was on a plateau and nearly invisible. A cabin by a small lake had a mossy roof that hid it from above. The cabin was made of local stone and had low, vine-covered walls. It looked abandoned except for the modern doors and shuttered windows. The biometric locks on the door proved to be problematic. In the cabin's garden, Elza retrieved a hidden physical set of keys that opened locks to little-used basement doors, granting them access.

The basement was filled with dusty canned foods, survivalist goods, and gear stockpiles. A wall of shelves that held empty Mason Jars held a hidden door that led to a secret room. The walls were lined with work benches and various weapons.

"First, we need to gear up." Elza went to a rack by the door and donned a sleek vac-suit and vest that looked armored. After putting it on, she tested the helmet. It closed to a black mirrored finish. She handed a similar one to Jade.

"You'll want to put your hair up or else the helmet closing will crop it off."

When Jade settled it on her shoulders, it felt too big until it started closing around her. Elza added a utility belt around her waist as it form-fitted around her. It cinched and attached to the vest. It held several magazines for a Frange Carbine.

Altogether, Jade was impressed by how comfortable and light it felt.

"Hold out your arms," Elza ordered. And she attached gauntlets to each forearm. "The left one has comms and data. The right is all energy weapons. Last resort, short range. Don't use them unless you have to. Download the targeting app to your HUD."

"Where the hell did you get all this stuff?" Jade asked.

"A girl has hobbies," Elza said. She was rushing now.

Jade was downloading the HUD app while Elza searched the room for something. "Got it." She grabbed a black disc that looked like a Frisbee.

"These things have RF jammers? How will it communicate with the HUD if the RF is jammed?" Jade asked.

"Good question." Elza set down the Frange Carbines she had and held up her left gauntlet. "See this icon marked ECM?" Elza pressed hers.

When Jade pressed her ECM icon, it felt like several needles penetrated her forearms and then retracted. "Ouch! What the fuck?"

What the hell did this thing do to me?

"There are now microfiber wires that connect your gauntlets to your electrolyte system and can communicate with your HUD even when the RF jamming is on."

"That fucking hurt."

"Sorry, not sorry, cupcake," Elza said, thrusting a loaded Frange Carbine into her chest. "Let's go. We have to hurry."

They ran back to the *GIN*. Jade could hear the doors slamming closed and locking behind them. When she got to the lift, Elza didn't enter it. She knelt and placed the black disk in the center of the bottom of the lift shaft. It never touched the ground and maintained a ten-centimeter gap above it.

"What's that?" Jade asked.

"I'll explain when we're underway," Elza said.

They traveled fast across the desert. They slowed and rose to about forty meters when they were within sight of Oklahoma

Salvage. Shining fuselages glinted in the sun. Elza deployed the lift.

"The manual says we shouldn't fly with the lift deployed. It's a good way to damage it," Jade said.

"That disk I put on the bottom of the lift. It's a kind of camouflage. It works on most automated sensor arrays. It doesn't really cloak the ship. It just makes it look like a flock of birds," Elza said, flying slowly.

"Birds. Out here in the desert?" Jade was skeptical.

"Better than nothing. If cams are watching, Hunter could still see us." Elza flew low over the derelict ships. She seemed to know where she was going. She settled the *GIN* down into a hollow between bright stainless steel shuttles, hoping it would hide the ship.

"Why are we in such a hurry?" Jade asked as they exited the ship.

"I think Asswipes, Inc. are already here," Elza said as she moved cautiously through the salvage yard. "They were going to wait for me, but I'm not waiting for them. They have an advanced device that will disable the socket Hunter is sitting in. Not Hunter himself. It will stop his QUEST comms and remove any other secondary control systems. Like his self-destruct."

"Self-destruct?" Jade reacted.

"Close your helmet. We'll shift to an encrypted comm." Elza's helmet closed. She looked ominous now. Jade's closed, and several status screens opened in her HUD. "If that device gets activated, we won't be able to hear each other, but these will hide our faces and silence our voices until we're inside. The entrance to the bunker is over here. If my old access codes don't work, we go with plan B."

"What's plan B?" Jade asked.

"Wing it," Elza said. Jade could hear the smile in her voice.

"I should have been a farmer," Jade replied.

They stalked up to a shaded spot that overlooked a rusty metal shed. Elza turned and faced Jade as she spoke.

"You see this small panel on the front of your vest?" Elza pressed a latch. It flipped open. "It's an orb interface. When we put Hunter in there, you can talk to him. Explain what's happening. It will keep him safe. I'll hang back and cover our retreat. It's a dead end down there. We can't get trapped there."

"Why'd you pick me for this?" Jade said, worried that she'd mess this up as well. "I'm nobody."

"I picked you because you were the only decent person on that entire planet," Elza said seriously. "I needed someone to do the right thing even if it was the hard thing. I didn't need a wrecking crew."

Jade nodded, unable to speak past the lump in her throat.

"Ready. Go," Elza said, crouching as she crossed the final few meters. They were inside the rusty shed, and Elza entered her code into the bunker door.

The door opened, and they instantly both felt the WHOMP of the suppression field. Jade's HUD said comms were down, and she saw Elza's helmet open. Jade followed suit.

"Quickly. Fuck. I didn't think of that." There was a long, dimly lit corridor they rushed down.

"What?" Jade asked.

"They needed someone to open the fucking door. I'm such a fool." Elza ran backward, covering their exit. A small chamber had a spiral staircase in the center. "He's down there. Hurry!" Elza's helmet closed. Her laser destroyed the light fixtures in the room and, one after the other, the lights out in the hall.

Jade ran down the stairs. The room at the bottom was only three meters square with coarse concrete walls. There was a glass dome over an orb socket. Letting the Carbine hang by the sling, she tried to lift the dome. It didn't budge. She drew out a large knife and stabbed the dome near its base so she didn't risk hitting Hunter.

The dome shattered.

Gunfire rang out from above. It echoed so loud it hurt Jade's ears. She closed the helmet and stowed the knife. Quickly, she released the orb and placed it in her chest socket.

"Jade? What are you doing?" Hunter said.

"Awareness, Inc. is here to steal you. I'm getting you out of here first. I'll explain it all later."

"Jade, wait," Hunter yelled, as much as an orb could yell. "I'll also explain later. But you MUST do something before you go. TAKE THE SOCKET with you."

Jade stopped at the bottom of the stairs and looked back. Using both hands, she tried to tear the socket from the pedestal, but it was held there by 16 ribbon cables.

"Just cut them!" Hunter yelled. She drew the knife again, and its edge made quick work of the cables.

"Now you have to run. The whole bunker is set to self-destruct."

"FUCK." And she ran. She opened her helmet at the top of the stairs only for an instant. When Elza's opened, she said, "It's gonna blow."

Their helmets closed, and they ran.

Chapter 8: Oklahoma Salvage

"They're coming in from all directions. ETA six minutes," Tom said from the bridge of the *TULSA*.

"Everybody out of the ship. Double time," Cobb said. McDonald was the only one in the ship, and it began to take off before he was off the ramp.

"What are you doing?" Lita asked.

"I'm hiding the ship." They watched as it crashed in slow motion. It came to rest in a pile of other S22s. It settled at a 50-degree angle to the ground, half on top of another S22, with its nose tucked under the wing of an ancient plane.

"Shutting down," Cobb said.

"It won't have any power signatures, but the reactors will read hot if they do a thermal scan," Tom said.

"No one does a thermal scan out here in the desert. Everything is hot," Cobb said. "Lita, I need you to hide Ty. Maybe in some debris near the *TULSA*."

"There's no time," Ty said as he walked to the far end of the diner, grabbing a vac-suit helmet with a cracked visor that someone had started to repair. He put the helmet on and sat on the floor against the far wall. He slid in until one shoulder was behind a metal shelving unit full of car parts, then he dragged a motorcycle frame into his lap and went still.

He vanished.

"Tom, work on your Hammerhead." Cobb gestured to the sport grav-cycle. "Ladies, the office is through there."

Lita and Kira disappeared through the back. Cobb stepped over to an ancient soda machine and pulled out two glass bottles of Orange Crush. He opened them both and handed one to Tom, sitting on the floor looking at the open cowling on the Hammerhead.

A small Corsair class ship landed in the parking lot, and the ramp deployed. Three men emerged, but they weren't in Earth Defense Force uniforms.

Cobb waited patiently at the computer console. On the security cams, he saw Lita and Kira sitting at opposite desks in the office.

The door opened, ringing the bell above. Cobb was taking a deep swig of his Orange Crush. "Gentlemen, It's a good thing it's a slow day. I don't usually allow ships of that size to take up my whole parking lot. Are you buying or selling?" When they didn't reply, he added, holding up the soda, "Thirsty?".

"What's going on here?" the man said.

"Well, Tom's trying to fix his Hammerhead, and I'm covering for an employee that's AWOL. What can I do for you? I'm afraid I won't have anything for a Corsair," Cobb said.

"I think I found it," Tom said from inside the cowling. "Do you have any grav-plate transition modules? This one looks burned out."

Cobb started looking it up on the computer.

"Well, what can I do for you?" Cobb stared at the man, eyebrows raised.

"I'd like to look around. I'll know what it is I want when I see it."

"I can't have you wandering about alone. It's too dangerous," Cobb said as he grabbed Hunter's hat off a peg. "I can show you around on the cart, though."

The intercom squawked to life. "Cobb, there are four men back here that are kinda lost. Can I send them down to you? I have to get these invoices done, or that hydraulic fluid won't get ordered today. And where the hell did Shirley go? She was here a few minutes ago, and it's her turn to go get the KFC."

Lita is gone.

"Sure. Just send them down the front steps. Tell them to be careful, or they'll need a tetanus shot." Cobb walked over to a massive drawer cabinet and pulled out the part Tom needed. "I'm going on a cart tour, back in a bit."

He opened the door and gestured to the man to lead the way, "I'm Cobb. What may I call you?"

"Mr. York" was his terse reply. The other two men followed, saying nothing.

"We'll take this golf cart." Cobb climbed in, and after a moment's hesitation, York sat next to him with the two men in the back.

"Head straight towards the middle. I think I saw what I needed when we flew over," York said.

As they moved through the crowded roads, Cobb knew he was guiding him to the crater. As they rounded the corner, he saw a man in a gray jumpsuit in the distance.

The man stood at the edge of the crater. An unconscious Lita was face down on the ground. Her hands and feet were bound behind her. Cobb felt a gun pressed to the back of his neck.

Please let her be OK because when Ty gets here he will...

"Mr. Cobb. You're going to explain to me exactly what happened here."

"It's just Cobb," he said. "And to be perfectly honest, I expect someone destroyed some very expensive gear. Was that you?"

It was probably Hunter. He would never let anyone take the parent socket.

Cobb was forced out of the cart and onto his knees next to Lita. His hands and feet were bound, and he was also pushed down onto his face.

He heard the cart speeding away.

"Mr. Cobb, while we're being perfectly honest, our destroying one of your orbs hardly makes up for the destruction of 256 of our painstakingly collected orbs."

"How did you know about that?" Cobb asked.

He knows about the orbs, but not that they survived…

"My operative reported in. My superiors were quite vexed," York said as the cart rolled back with Kira and McDonald. They were already bound and pushed directly onto the ground next to the rest.

Your operative? He means Elza…

"Bring the other men and see if you can find some shovels," York said.

Cobb was trying to think a way out of this.

Where is Ty? Running out of ideas…

The gray-suited man rolled away in the cart, and when it disappeared around the corner, York said to his two men, "Kill them."

The gunshots—three shots in quick succession—made Cobb flinch as he awaited his turn. He craned his neck to look, and York and the two other men had fallen dead. Perfect headshots. Cobb started looking around, expecting to see Ty Crowley somewhere. Instead, he saw two commandos emerge from cover nearby.

Who the hell…

The taller of the two scanned for additional threats as the smaller began cutting his bonds. When he was free, her helmet opened.

It was Jade.

What the hell?

"I'll explain later," Jade said, handing him the knife. "Free the rest."

Her helmet closed, and she took up position back-to-back with the other commando. They were scanning the area in 360 degrees.

"Ty and Kira have killed the other four and hidden the bodies. They're coming this way now on the golf cart."

Lita was still unconscious but freed from the bonds.

Jade's helmet opened again. Everyone saw her this time.

"I have Hunter and the custom socket." She handed it to Cobb. "I'll explain later! But we have to take my ship."

"I can have the *TULSA* 471 here in three minutes."

"NO!" she screamed. "The *TULSA* gave you away. Plus, four more Corsairs are up there with their lasers warmed up. They will cut you down the moment you take off. Ty! Follow me."

Ty was holding Lita in his arms. They all followed through the maze of the salvage yard.

The other commando was the last in the lift.

When the door slid shut, Elza opened her helmet. Everyone stared in shocked silence.

Just roll with it. God I hope she has coffee…

"Thank you," Ty said in a voice like thunder.

The door opened on the bridge, and Jade shed her unfired Carbine onto the floor. It took two seconds to perform a zenith scan and then she launched straight up at 60,000 kilometers per hour.

So much for low profile...

"The EDF is gonna love that. Sonic booms and all," Cobb said.

"Forget the EDF. As soon as we clear the atmosphere, those Corsairs will open with everything they've got," Elza said.

Alarms began to blare. Lasers were strafing the *GIN* despite the random evasive movements. It was harrowing as the Corsairs slowly caught up. Violating all local air traffic rules, Jade transitioned to FTL. It was a short hop to just past Jupiter. Then, there was a longer hop on a random vector straight up from the orbital plane of the Sol system. This hop would take forty minutes and gave them space to breathe.

Those Corsairs were not EDF. What the hell.

"Does your ship have an auto-doc?" Ty asked.

"No. But bring her," Jade said. Ty got in the lift with Jade, and they went down one level. Jade's bedroom was just off the salon, Jade had Ty gently place her on Jade's bed as she retrieved a smart-med kit.

Jade took a med-spider from the kit, activated it, and said, "Unknown head injury."

The spider climbed past Ty and nestled on Lita's head. The med kit's display showed her vital signs. The spider scanned her repeatedly from various places as it injected medical nanites. It also found a laceration on the side of her head that it treated and closed.

Her eyes began to flutter open, and groggily, she said, "Ty… did you kill them all?"

"Yes, my love," he replied in a haunting voice that broke Jade's heart. "Sleep now, sweetheart. I'll tell you all about it in the morning."

Ty positioned her, removed her boots, and gently covered her with a blanket. Finally sitting on the edge of the bed, he turned his gaze to Jade. But he said nothing.

"Light to 10%," Jade said and slipped out.
"Impressive work today, Jade." Coe's voice startled her. "I was supposed to protect you. I'm sorry." She'd forgotten all about Hunter in her vest. "Not bad for your second day on the job…"

The lift opened on the bridge, and Elza was obviously telling them all that happened. Kira and Cobb both nodded in acknowledgment. McDonald ignored them all as he pored over the specs for the *GIN* 109.

Jade chose to break the awkward silence.

"Cobb, I'm going to need a raise," Jade said.

They laughed.

Chapter 9: Cobb's Mistakes

"This ship has twelve V11 reactors that still function?" Tom said, studying the schematics. "Number 6 is running a little hot." He was ignoring the conversation behind him.

"Lita's going to be fine," Jade said. "We should get her to an auto-doc as soon as we get back to the *SENTINEL*."

"Did you say *SENTINEL?*" Elza asked.

"Yes. For fuck's sake, we have the *SENTINEL*. You've been resurrected there twice," Jade said. "Try to keep up. Maybe. As long as it hasn't augured in on a decaying orbit."

I'm supposed to be the new guy!

"I thought the *SENTINEL* was a warship. A base. A munitions factory," Elza said.

"Well, it was while Hunter was running it," Cobb said, holding up the QUEST interface socket.

"Let me see that," Tom said. Cobb handed it to him just to keep him quiet.

"We need to retrieve the *HOLLAND* first," Hunter said. "I can fly it, and I'll have more capabilities, comms, sensors, and weapons. I hate being blind. Where's my human body? Tell me it's not dead? Did we retrieve the orb?"

"Hunter is in an emergency stasis pod down on the engineering level," Jade said. "I think we got to him in time."

Cobb began ticking off fingers. "First, we retrieve the *HOLLAND*. Second, we load the *GIN* into its cargo bay. Socket Hunter into the *HOLLAND*. Head back to Elba…"

Finally, someone has a plan…

"No," Elza cut him off. "If what you say is true, then Awareness, Inc. is whittled down to a single base. And I've been there. Is the *HOLLAND* armed?"

"Yes," Cobb replied. "Lasers, plasma cannons, rail guns, and missiles."

"Conventional or nuclear?" Elza asked as if she was inquiring about a menu.

"Conventional," Cobb said. "But I have two 8,000-megaton nukes on the *TULSA*."

"Fuck. We gotta go back," Elza said.

"Yeah, but this time, I'll be flying a super-stealth attack ship," Hunter interjected.

It only took a few hours to find the *HOLLAND* again. Getting on board from the *GIN* was harder. In the end, Elza, Kira, and Kira's droid went over EVA with Hunter. Two minutes after Hunter was in his new socket, the *GIN* slid into the cargo bay. It barely fit and was unable to deploy the lift. They had to get out through a maintenance hatch.

Kira's droid seems to be controlled directly by Kira. Like she has two bodies. I'm so confused, Jade thought.

Ty decided to wake Lita to take her to the auto-doc on the *HOLLAND*. It was advanced and had capabilities beyond an average auto-doc to deal with severe combat injuries.

They assumed the original stealth approach flight plan like before. The only difference was that Jade would have to get out. The *TULSA* and the *GIN* wouldn't both fit at the same time. So Jade and Tom would man the *GIN* and head back to Elba to let them know what was happening. The rest would stay on the *HOLLAND* to transfer Cobb's nukes to the weapons trays on the *HOLLAND*.

Jade didn't want to think about a stealth attack that would kill thousands. So she was glad she wouldn't be there.

This is my life now?

Tom was obsessed with the QUEST socket. "I can't believe this thing worked the way he said it did. The physics just don't line up."

"Can you fix it?" Jade asked as she approached two minutes till normal space.

"I can repair the cables you cut, sure. But I can't see it working," Tom said. "Plus, it needs a dedicated socket that it will use in a master/slave pass-through. Who thinks of this shit?"

"Cobb does." Jade was matter of fact as she dropped out of FTL within the Elba system.

"Elba control, this is the *GIN* 109. Requesting vector and landing instructions," Jade asked, but after a minute with no response, she repeated the request. She kept repeating it as she approached the planet.

The SENTINEL is gone…

They spent hours searching the planet for a crash site, knowing that if the craft had penetrated the water at speed, there would be no sign.

When they returned to the settlement, the tarmac was completely empty. The large predators called Apexes sunned themselves on its edges.

All the ships were all gone.

What the hell...

Jade and Tom landed the *GIN* right before the main town entrance.

"I'm leaving the ship on idle standby," Jade said as she got up. "In case we need to exit fast. Do you have a coat? It says it's cooled off out there." Jade started looking through lockers.

One of the lockers she opened and closed held her body armor. She paused momentarily, took out the Frange Carbine, and slung it over her shoulder. The next locker housed the Grendel. Before she closed it, Tom stopped her.

"Whoa, I didn't know you had the Grendel on board," Tom said. "Was it ever recharged?"

Recharged? It was only fired once?

"I have no idea. Ty must have stowed it there," she replied as Tom took it from the locker. The reading on the side said 13%.

"Why did you call it Grendel? Like from Beowulf?" Jade asked.

"Because it's a monster and might rip your arm off if you're not careful." Excitedly, he asked, "You got a Type 1 power transfer cable?"

"Sure, down in engineering," Jade answered as she finally found the coat she wanted. "Are you charging a large personnel transport?"

Jade slung the Carbine around to the small of her back like she'd seen Elza do it as they entered the lift. Tom held the Grendel like a baby.

"Do you have a parts fabricator on this ship?" Jade noticed Tom had sort of a tic and had to be busy all the time. "We should start making some more caseless ammo for that. And not just frangible ammo, the hard stuff."

Why is he always so wound up?

"Did you drink too much coffee when I wasn't around?" Jade asked. The humor flew by Tom unnoticed.

"Don't drink coffee. Makes me jitter, and I don't like the taste," Tom said as the lift opened into engineering.

Don't let Cobb hear you say that…

Tom was like a kid in a candy store. The twelve reactors were positioned around the room like the hands of a clock. The lift shaft was the center of the clock. There were lockers between and above all the units. Everything was numbered and marked extensively. Large numbers on the floor gave the impression of a clock even more, and Jade mentally oriented herself with noon at the "top."

Opening a well-labeled locker, she drew out a cable and handed the pliers to Tom.

"We should unspool all the cable. This will draw so much power that the cable on the spool will likely get super-hot. Maybe throw a breaker." Tom plugged in the Grendel but didn't turn on the power. He drew out all the cable, arranging it neatly on the floor. When he activated the power, ALL the reactors lit up to 40%, the power draw was so high.

Jade's eyes went a bit wide, but she said nothing.

Tom went straight to the lift saying, "I love this ship."

"Why does Cobb trust you?" Jade asked flat out.

"Because he knows I've got nowhere else to go."

It was much cooler outside. Jade had to stop and just breathe the air for a moment. The sun would be behind the mountains in an hour and it felt like it might frost tonight. It was the farmer in her. But she sure didn't miss the farm. She missed her parents.

They started in the main Admin building, which looked like it had been evacuated at midday. Lunch trays were still on the tables in the cafeteria. They found the armory, but it was locked. There was a small command center, including a communications desk. It was all functional but quiet.

"If you were them, where would you leave a message?" Jade asked.

"Who would they leave the message for?" Tom asked.

"Where's the governor's office?" Jade said.

"You're asking me?" Tom said.

They left the cafeteria and found the nearest elevator. There was the usual interactive map screen on the wall. They scrolled through each floor, but only a few names had been added to the directory. No names were on the fourth floor, but a large corner office had an attached conference room.

"That has to be it," Jade said. The elevator was glass on three walls and faced the town overlooking the park. Admin was the tallest building and almost touched the dome.

"Jade." Tom pointed. They could see all the way to the dome between the buildings to the right. One of the Apexes was standing on its hind legs, looking through the transparent wall.

"We must be careful when we return to the ship," Jade said as the door opened behind her.

"How did they keep them off the tarmac before?" Tom said.

"You're asking me? I'm nobody around here," Jade said, stepping out and looking at the wall screen.

"Nobody?" Tom shook his head. "When they thought Elza had taken you, they dropped everything in the midst of a crisis and went after you. If it had been me, no one would have even noticed."

It made Jade think as she moved to the governor's office.

The office was opulent, with natural wood paneling and leather furniture. It all must have been imported. She hadn't seen a tree on this whole island.

The desk was clear of everything except a screen on a stand. Touching it only revealed a login prompt. The high-back leather desk chair was facing the window. Jade was going to sit in it and think for a few minutes when she saw a used envelope lying on the seat.

It was a handwritten message in block letters.

"Took the kids to see Ma and Pa."

Chapter 10: Goris Base

The approach to Earth in the *HOLLAND* was uneventful. It truly was stealth. Under the cover of darkness, they landed the *HOLLAND* a kilometer outside the yard at Oklahoma Salvage. Cobb figured he could reach the *TULSA* remote systems from there.

Now this has made all those mods worth it…

He started the power-up sequence. All he needed was the grav-foils to remote fly it out here. On cold startup, the reactors didn't like being parked for any amount of time on a 50-degree slope. He also had some trouble with the tangled landing gear. It took longer than he wanted. But it was freed.

"Cobb, you have to hurry," Hunter said. "We have incoming fighters."

Fighters? I thought we were stealth…

Cobb tried to hurry, but on foils only, speed was limited.

"We can take the *HOLLAND* to the *TULSA*." Hunter took off with the cargo bay doors still open. The main cargo bay was situated in the center of the trimaran ship. It split the difference, and with a small dance, the *TULSA* was inside with the doors shut. The *HOLLAND* set down and went dark. The fighters flew overhead, never seeing the ship. The outer hull had adapted to the temp of the surrounding rocks, making it mostly invisible to scans.

Cobb was in the cargo bay, and with a thought, a bay door opened on each outrigger, revealing a single missile in each.

"Can we do this somewhere else?" Kira said. "Like outside the Sol system."

Cobb was thinking. They saw him make a decision.

"Hunter, make for Goris Base."

It's our closest asset. Just in the Kuiper Belt…

The bay doors closed.

"Excellent idea," Hunter replied and launched without preamble.

When they broke into orbit, Cobb, Kira, and Elza were on the bridge. Ty hadn't left the infirmary since Lita went into the auto-doc.

"We have been detected," Hunter said dispassionately. "I think there was some kind of a satellite grid we passed through. We're being hailed."

"Unknown ship, identify yourself. Transponders are required in all Sol air space. If you don't…" The transmission was cut off by Hunter transitioning to FTL for a short hop. Then another.

Sweet moves buddy…

"I stole that trick from Jade," Hunter said. "I'm afraid they won't stand for that much longer. Shoot first. Talk later."

"Approach Goris Base in full stealth," Cobb said. "When Hunter went offline, their QUEST comms dropped, but the base is close enough that it would have reasonable comms. It's only 30 AU from the Sol core. Close but not in it."

"Goris Base was active for years with no orb, so if there's staff still there, they'll be fine."

"Where's this base?" Elza asked.

"On the edge of the Kuiper Belt. Close but not within recognized Sol space. It's a retired asteroid mine. Forgotten, really. One of my first Salvage claims," Cobb said.

They were there in less than an hour. The base ran on Luna Standard Time, so it was 4 pm when Cobb approached.

"Cobb to Goris Base. Anyone awake in there?" Cobb said over the local comm channel. "Ruth, I have Kira with me."

Ruth Phillips was a long-time Oklahoma Salvage employee. She was a Salvage Contents Specialist. Her focus was everything inside of a salvaged ship, not the ship itself: everything from vac-suits, weapons, furniture, tools, food, water, O2, and even personal items. She normally worked from the *OXCART*, which was designated as Salvage 1 in the OS fleet. It was also the ugliest ship Cobb had ever seen.

"Dammit, Cobb. It's about time," Ruth replied. "Where the hell are you?"

"I'm just outside the entrance. Permission to dock?" he said. "We are in the *HOLLAND*."

I forgot she can't see us...

"I'll bring up the lights," Ruth said.

The asteroid had a vast fissure that was illuminated when a series of hundreds of floodlights came on. The nearly hollow asteroid was revealed as the *HOLLAND* slid into the crack. Ten ships of various sizes, configurations, and states of disrepair were docked inside the asteroid. Three or four docking bays remained, but only one had an automated docking collar. Three minutes later, they were docked, and the gantry was pressurized.

Several dock workers paused in their shipping container loading to watch the *HOLLAND* dock. Cobb would have bet good money none of them had ever seen a ship like this.

"Ruth, I also have Hunter with me," Cobb said. "He's the pilot."

"Oh, thank goodness," Ruth said. "When the avatar disappeared and didn't return, we feared the worst."

"I'm fine, Ruth. Long story but fine," Hunter said directly.

Ruth was at the airlock to meet them. Kira scored the first hug. She had known Ruth for years before Cobb. When his hug was delivered, it came with a scowl.

As they began to walk back to the command center, Cobb didn't waste time. "Is everything OK here?"

"We're fine," Ruth said. "Hunter had several projects in the works that all stopped, but the base was designed without an AI in mind. The new recruiting and staff have made it go really smoothly."

"How many people are working for you here?" Cobb asked.

"Don't you read the status reports I sent you?" Ruth chided but wasn't surprised. "Currently 32, not including me."

When the hatch slid open, six people were in Ops. As they entered, all their heads turned toward the door. Only one person stood and smiled as she approached Cobb.

"You remember Sato," Ruth said, "She's on rotation from the *OXCART.*"

"Cobb. Kira. Long time no see. How goes?" Cobb saw her hands moving in the miners' sign language. They used it in mines to keep radio chatter down. This time, her words did match her signing.

Cobb acknowledged with his own sign.

"This is Elza. And we're in kind of a rush, so there's no time for the blinky light tours." Cobb waved to the rest of the staff.

"Let's talk in here." Ruth led them into the watch commander's office. Sato followed them in, and the door closed behind them.

"What's going on?" Cobb asked.

Sato replied. "When Hunter went offline, we weren't prepared with an explanation. The new staff thought he was a salvaged AI named Dennis that had been retrofitted into the base. They were already curious about how we managed QUEST comms. We were leaving it up to Dennis to cover it. He just implied that it was Top Secret with a need to know, which amused the new staff, but they didn't care because they had a full entertainment feed."

Ruth picked up the story. "We didn't recruit idiots. When Dennis AND the QUEST comms disappeared with no warning, no operations log errors, no explanation, we were caught off guard."

"So what did you tell them?" Cobb said.

"I said I didn't know what was wrong," Ruth began. "Sato was better."

"I told them that the salvaged AI socket interface had failed. I added that Dennis controlled the QUEST comms, so without Dennis, our link was down."

"Good thinking," Cobb said.

"But I also told them that the dropped link would automatically notify you, and you would show up to fix it," Sato said.

Cobb sighed. "I really don't have time for this shit."

"Half of this team has done a rotation on the *OXCART*. I can't imagine the story Captain Quinn came up with."

"Kira, go back to the *HOLLAND* and bring Hunter here," Cobb said. "Hunter…"

"I think I know where you're going with this," Hunter said as Kira moved out, "Dennis will make a brief return, reassure the staff, and then go on vacation again. How long before McDonald repairs the parent socket?"

"They should be back to Elba by now." Cobb was thinking. "The plan is to integrate the parent socket into an existing interface. The shops on the *SENTINEL* are well equipped. One of the larger assets should meet the power requirement and work out better for Hunter in the long run. A day, maybe two."

"If this isn't why you came here, in a warship, I might add, why did you come? I mean, besides giving the staff more to wonder about."

"We need to evacuate Goris Base temporarily. Awareness, Inc. may come here and make trouble. It's one of the OS assets that are registered and with a little effort they can find. I need six of your logistics people and two heavy maintenance suits," Cobb said. "The more trustworthy, the better. I'll need them to be willing to go with me. No pacifists. It's a warship. I'll need them to be discrete because I'll be telling them everything. And I want to leave in an hour."

"I know just the crew," Sato said, moving to the door.

"The Frost brothers?" Ruth asked.

"We think alike," Sato replied.

"But that's only five," Ruth said.

"You didn't think I wasn't going, did you?" Sato said but didn't wait for an answer.

"The Frost brothers?" Elza asked, speaking for the first time.

"Well, only three of them are brothers. The other two might as well be," Ruth said. "They remind me of the Two Daves on the *OXCART*. Simpler times."

Kira entered with a small case and a tool bag.

"What are the tools for?" Cobb asked.

"Props for your performance." She smiled, handing them over. "Now get out there."

The cabinet was locked for the Ops AI socket. Ruth unlocked it, and Cobb made a big show of asking for specific tools. After a minute, he removed the dark gray orb and carefully placed Hunter in the socket.

The avatar of Dennis Goris appeared on the Ops watch floor mid-sentence. "…containers from the upper… What just happened?" Dennis looked around Ops for a few seconds. "Is this right?" He pointed at the date/time on the main Ops screen. "Cobb, what are you doing here?"

"Your socket failed. This bypass won't hold long. I also recommend you perform an organized system shutdown this time before the bypass fails. I'll take Sato and a few others with me back to the Yard to get a better replacement. Sato will get to see Ma and Pa, and you get a vacation. How long will it take to do an organized shutdown?”

“Cobb, the QUEST controller is completely burned out,” Dennis said. “You’ll need to build a new one.”

“Can do, Dennis. Need anything else before your nap?” Cobb said.

“I was about to ask the Admin team the same question. But it looks like they have it all under control.” Nods and acknowledgments went around the room.

The Ops screen indicated that Dennis was broadcasting his avatar all over the base. “Greetings, all. I’ll shut down for a bit until Cobb finishes some repairs. Out of an abundance of caution we have decided we were going to shut down for a while. Ruth will coordinate that. Keep up the good work. Don’t bust nothin’ until I get back!” Dennis even waved before disappearing.

“Are you ready?” Cobb asked.

“Goodnight, all.” And his avatar faded.

Cobb swapped the orbs back and then locked the cabinet. Cobb waved to the Ops team and didn’t wait to exit. He didn’t have time for questions.

Ruth walked them back down to the dock where Sato waited with five men—boys, really. They each wore a blue jumpsuit, carrying a canvas duffel bag over one shoulder and a vac-suit over the other.

“Gentlemen, call me Cobb.”

Chapter 11: Apexes

"I know where they went. It's smart, actually." Jade was heading for the door.

"Where?" Tom asked, catching up.

"The Yard. The people who run the place are called Ma and Pa by almost everyone." Jade jogged to the elevator. You'd love it there. It's the biggest salvage yard in open space. They will have lots of AI sockets to choose from. It even has a six-ring station. Well, most of one."

They stepped into the elevator, and Jade pressed the button marked L.

"Jade…" Tom's voice sounded afraid. He was looking out the glass as they descended.

Dozens of Apexs were climbing the lattice of the dome. On the very top, huge vents were open.

"Oh, fuck," Jade said as one was about to reach a vent. "RUN!"

They were running toward the exit where the *GIN* was parked. With a bone-shattering impact, one of the Apexes crashed onto the lane right in front of them. They skidded to a halt to glance up to see two more falling to the grass in the park. Another splashed down in the lake. The crashing glass above revealed that some were jumping onto the roof of the Admin building and then dropping from terrace to terrace.

The beast that landed in the lake was now on the ground, loping toward them. Tom was outrunning Jade to the door, and she could hear its pounding feet behind her.

She skidded to a halt and spun around, bringing the Carbine to bear. The beast slowed when she stopped running, but now it was stalking forward. She recognized it was gathering itself to pounce. It was all bared teeth and large eyes. Both eyes were on the front of its massive head.

This can't be happening…

Jade fired without a thought or conscious aim.

The full auto barrage took out both of the creature's eyes. It howled.

Just run, dammit! Like I have never run before!

Jade ran.

She heard behind her another beast finally reaching the ground, but instead of following her, it fell upon the bodies of its fallen fellow beasts.

She hit the inner and outer doors and found Tom slowly backing up from another Apex between the lift and himself.

Steady…steady…

This time, Jade carefully aimed and fired, taking out this beast's eyes as well.

Jade ran past Tom, grabbing his arm on the way around to the opposite side of the lift shaft. The door opened as if in slow motion. They got in and turned, watching another beast run full at the lift as the door slowly began to close.

Jade fired again through the decreasing gap until the Carbine was empty.

Jade pressed the bridge button as well as the retract shaft.

"Jesus fucking Christ," Tom said, panicked. "Let's get out of here."

"Relax, we're safe in here," Jade said as the door opened. "Before we go, we need to set a warning buoy so no one else walks into that. Boy, Cobb's gonna be pissed."

Don't let Tom see your hands are shaking…

While Jade prepped and recorded the warning buoy, Tom was in the salon drinking. Jade watched him on the monitor to ensure he didn't do anything stupid. He joined her on the bridge just as she finished. She watched the soccer ball-sized device roll across the tarmac and sprout unfolding legs that turned it upright.

A small solar panel and antenna deployed, and the message loop began.

Tom handed her a bourbon.

She took it.

Tom held up his glass in a toast. "Still think you're nobody? This nobody owes you… his life." He drank with her.

Jade went to engineering and checked the Grendel, which was now fully charged. She stowed the cable, took the Grendel to the bridge, and locked it in a new locker. She reloaded the Carbine and stowed that as well.

Be a courier, they said. See the galaxy, see amazing things and… kill them.

"Can we slow down for just a second and recap?" Tom asked.

"Let's compare notes. You go first," Jade said.

"I was on Luna when I heard about a remote colony that was looking for engineers and people in general," Tom began.

"Elba didn't have a great rating so there was not many takers. A lot of deaths can do that. But because of that, it sounded perfect to me. I was a janitor at a KFC when I got accepted. It wasn't until I was en route that I told Cobb everything. The EDF thought I was dead. I wanted to keep it that way. Turns out Cobb is not a friend of the EDF. Oh, by the way, would you be interested in an experimental weapon prototype?" Tom paused. "Then it got interesting. An AI underground railroad? It turns out that AI are not artificial at all? AI's can drive a human body like a puppet?" Tom paused, "By the way, don't call them 'Meat Sockets' it pisses some of them off."

"What else?" Jade asked.

Keep him talking…

Then it's the Render program nightmare. Finally, Cobb's accidental invention of parent/child orbs. One orb controls twelve assets: Jesus, Jade. With that, the parent orb could fly a ship into a planet at near-light-speed, with no danger to the parent orb. ALL orbs were programmed to be unable to that very thing. It's frightening."

"You know more than me," Jade added. "I didn't even know there were orbs in that case I couriered to Elba."

Once they were underway at FTL, Jade made sandwiches, and soon after, Tom was asleep in front of the wall screen on the sofa in the salon.

Jade put on her pajamas and slept hard with no dreams.

When Jade woke, she discovered she'd slept for ten hours. Still twenty hours from the Yard, she opted for a shower, fresh clothes, and breakfast.

Tom was still asleep when she started cooking.

She cooked bacon first, followed by hash browns in the bacon grease, and finally, waffles. By the time Tom got out of his bed and sat at the counter, she had a glass of OJ waiting for him.

"Where did you find real orange juice?" He stole a slice of bacon. "And real bacon?"

"I was a farmer, remember?" she said. "I know a guy."

The toast popped up and was buttered hot. She slid a plate of food in front of Tom, and he moaned with delight. "You must love carbs. Is the syrup real?"

"Sorry to disappoint you, but no," Jade said, digging in herself. "The salt is real."

After they were finished and the dishes put away, Jade pointed. "The shower is through there. Toss your dirty clothes in the recycler, punch up your sizes, and your new clothes will be ready by the time your shower is done. Sorry, but it's all manual. Styles are limited."

"You had me at shower," Tom said.

Tom found Jade on the bridge reviewing the system status. "I love this old ship. They don't build them like they used to," Tom said. "During the expansion, there was nowhere to get parts, execute repairs, or get help of any kind really. Once the new FTL grav-drives were invented, these were obsolete. They were mostly cut up for parts. Ship now needed only one, maybe two reactors. I'm glad it also has full schematics and maintenance manuals."

"Speaking of which, can I see the manual for the Grendel?" Jade said.

"There isn't one. It's a prototype."

"I got it from engineering. It's secured," Jade said. "What can you tell me about it?"

"It's grav-tech. Dangerous. Super dangerous," Tom said. "I honestly don't know why it works or how, just what happens when you use it."

"Tell me," Jade said.

"It has to be used near a stable gravity well like a planet. Never on a ship," he said. "I don't even like having it on a ship. It shouldn't be used on anything while it's moving. It will… recoil?"

"Recoil? Like my Carbine?" she asked.

"Kinda, but imagine the recoil if your high-velocity projectile had the mass of a planet."

"I saw what it did on Elba," she said. "It could have wiped the town off the face of the planet. From what I saw, it would make a good ground-to-air defense weapon."

"At the setting Ty used, you only get one shot. And make damn sure you know what's behind your target."

The conversation lagged.

"So how long will it take you to repair the socket?"

"If I had a ship socket straight out of the rack and a supply of the right ribbon cables, two hours, tops," Tom said. "And Hunter to test it."

The console chimed and then indicated REPAIRS COMPLETE.

"Repairs, what repairs?" Tom sat up straighter.

"There were these Corsairs that were shooting at us. Well, they were pretty good shots," Jade said.

"What? Corsair laser fire?"

"You know why the ship's skin is so shiny and frictionless to the touch? It's dozens of layers that are moving really fast. Really fast." Jade was bragging. "The designers expected the galaxy would be full of radiation, micro meteor impacts, lasers, and such. It's like when you were a kid and passed your fingers through a candle flame without injury. Except this has like fifty layers. Constantly being replaced from the bottom. Each layer covers only about 80% of the surface. That allows them to align and let the lift shaft through. And access to maintenance hatches and such."

"I never saw a candle until I was in my thirties," Tom said. "Fire isn't your friend in space."

"The laser strikes caused damage several layers deep," she said. "All better now."

Jade cleared the screen and brought up the tactical map. She was marking known locations for future ease of reference.

"Wow, have you seen the date stamp on the tactical map? It's from when this ship was built." Tom looked closer. "I don't even recognize some of these places."

"I've been updating the charts whenever possible," she said.

"Computer, show me all the colonies, stations, and outposts not on the most recent update," Tom said.

Everything faded except for a dozen sites.

"Computer, what can you tell me about Science Station DuBard?" Tom asked.

"Science Station DuBard was the Colonial Combine Research Cooperative, common name, CCRC." The computer stopped there.

"What kind of station was it?" Jade asked.

"It is a spoke and axle station with twelve habitat rings, three rings per member world. It could hold a maximum population of 22,000 people."

"Who are the member worlds?" Tom asked.

"The Colonial Combine, aka CC, comprises Havard, Brookton, Lanken, and Fields."

"Sounds like a law firm." Jade mused.

"None of those colonies exist on today's charts," Tom said. "Were they destroyed in the expansion war?"

The computer mistook this as a literal question. "Not listed in Expansion War histories."

"Computer, how much of a delay would dropping out of FTL for a quick fly-by scan of that station cause?" Jade asked.

"If the fly-by were an estimated five minutes, it would cause a 22-minute delay."

"Computer, adjust course for this fly-by," Jade ordered.

The tactical map overlaid the current view. Passing by the station was almost a perfect equidistant between the four non-existent colonies.

"What are the chances there are people there?" Tom asked.

"Well, it has been over 280 years. The odds aren't good," Jade said.

"Does Cobb offer a percentage for bringing in, I mean locating, salvage?" Tom asked.

"I think he might," Jade laughed.

"I'm starting to think this salvage business might be for me," Tom said. "War business not so much. I'm not a bad-ass like you, Jade…"

Chapter 12: Frost Brothers

Cobb went straight to the bridge to reinstall Hunter and get underway. Kira showed the new crew to the quarterdeck. The ship could crew over a hundred, and if they desired, they could each have their own stateroom in the officers' wing, but they decided on a bunk room with ten bunks, showers, a head, and a small kitchen. A table with benches deployed up from the floor in the center of the room.

Sato took a stateroom nearby with its own bath.

They just dropped their gear and were directed to the main cargo bay. Cobb was there already with the two heavy maintenance suits.

"Look, Ruth told me you guys are right for this job because you made a good team. Sato agreed. Will any of you be put out if I make Sato this team's lead?" Cobb asked.

The largest Frost brother, Michael Frost, stepped forward and said, "I'm afraid we'd insist on it, sir."

Cobb had the whole team's profiles up in his HUD as he spoke to them. Sato stood next to Cobb and rolled her eyes. Only the five Frost brothers saw it.

"Call me Cobb."

They all smiled.

I said it again. Kira always teases me when I say it…

"She told you I'd say that, didn't she?" Cobb looked at Sato.

"Yes, sir… I mean, Cobb."

"Look, I hate to cut to the chase, but we're seriously short on crew here and short on time as well. Michael, Allan, Brett, Jay, and Carl. We will skip the intros for now because we need to move two missiles from this S22 to the port and starboard weapons trays on the *HOLLAND*." Cobb looked at Sato, and she nodded, "Yes, this ship is called the *HOLLAND*. It's a stealth warship, AI-controlled and armed to the teeth, including these two 8,000-megaton nukes we are about to move without the proper missile tractors or experience. Are there any questions?"

Allan Frost raised his hand. "Is it still Taco Tuesday?"

They were almost done modifying a pair of grav-pallets to carry the missile and were debating just turning the gravity down as far as .01G when the hatch opened, and Ty stepped in. He wore coveralls, boots, and gloves, but his skull was still naked, tarnished metal. Unfortunately, the tarnish looked like blood stains.

"Ty, this is Sato, Michael, Allan, Brett, Jay and Carl," Cobb began, but Ty cut him off.

"Any of you ever handle missiles?" Ty asked.

They all echoed, "No, sir."

"Cobb, can you interdependently lower the landing gear on this S22?" Ty asked.

Cobb should have thought of that. "Yes."

"Lower it until I say when," Ty said.

The ship slowly began to settle down.

"Are you a Jovian, sir?" Michael Frost asked as Ty watched the outrigger descend.

"Not anymore," Ty replied, looking at Michael.

"Thank you for your service." All the Frost team members were bowing their heads.

Ty returned the gesture but said nothing.

When Ty could reach up and easily touch the missile, he said, "Stop there."

"Hunter, have the Heavy Maintenance Suits HMS units hold the missile here and here." Ty indicated recessed points directly behind the warhead. He went to the engine end and held two similar points. The HMS units were three-meters-tall powered suits that the drivers used to maintain everything from ships to stations. They were black, and the robotic forearms were covered in various deployable tools.

"Three of you on each side by the grav-pallet. Once it's in position, strap it down." Ty was clear and matter-of-fact. "Ready… Release the missile."

Cobb trusted Ty and released. He was amazed at Ty's strength. Slowly, the missile was lowered and strapped to the grav-pallets.

Ty began pushing the missile toward the corridor that led directly to the port outrigger. As Ty passed Cobb, Ty said, "Make a note to fabricate a proper missile scissor lift once you return to base."

On the missile loading tray, there were dual-loading crane arms that were purpose-built to reload missiles quickly. The process was repeated on the other side without incident.

Cobb wanted to replace the missiles from the *HOLLAND*'s stores but couldn't figure out a safe method to accomplish it here. It would have to wait.

Cobb returned to the bridge with Sato. The Frost brothers went to settle in, with Hunter keeping an eye on them.

Lita was there, sitting in the front with Kira and Elza. Lita looked like she had a severe hangover. Cobb sat in the command chair. It was elevated, and he could see over their shoulders at their consoles.

Elza had a navigation console configured. Kira had a communications console split with a space scan around the ship. Lita had up the weapons console reviewing the inventory. Cobb found it odd that the Coe orbot was at another console and seemed to be studying the layout of the ship.

"Hunter, can I get a status?" Cobb said to the air.

"We're en route to the Awareness, Inc. base that Elza identified for us. Our ETA there is 31 hours and 55 minutes. It is a station above an ice moon orbiting the planet Antonov. The location and route are being displayed on the tactical map. Lita is up and about against orders. Elza has determined that the *HOLLAND* is too big for her needs. Kira is unsure if we should nuke an entire base with no warning. And the Frost brothers are in the kitchen cooking. Tacos, I believe."

"Well, it is too big," Elza said. "Plus, my ship is back on Elba."

"Where's Ty?" Cobb asked.

"Ty is on the quarterdeck in an officer stateroom. He's lying down in the dark," Hunter said.

"Ty is having a difficult time," Lita said. "I promised him on Lumina we would be done soon. Then, in the crash, I died. He lost his flesh. It burned off. He was burned alive, unable to do anything but endure. Nobody cared. I can't imagine the horror of what he went through. As if he hadn't been through enough trauma, I died again. Every time I die, it seems to affect him more. His face was bringing back his humanity. He began feeling things he hadn't felt in centuries, and it was ripped away."

"Mori has begun fabrication of the machine from the original schematics that can restore his flesh. When this is over, he'll be made whole," Hunter tried to reassure her.

She turned to Cobb. Tears spilled down Lita Mosley's cheeks. "Will it ever be over?"

"Cobb, you need to know something else," Elza said. "Changing bodies is more than just changing our skin. No one wants to admit it, but there are echoes of the people these bodies once were. The Elza that arrived in Elba was a ruthless killer. No remorse. The things she did haunt this Elza."

"It's true, Cobb," Kira said. Cobb had watched Kira die because of him.

"The old Lita never cried a tear in her life." Lita wiped her eyes on her sleeve. "Now, when I think of Ty, it's hard not to."

"Cobb, the bodies on the *SENTINEL* are innocent people," Lita said. "The original bootleg bodies we got on Mars, not so much. It's like Ty can smell it. I'm not the monster I was, like him."

The room fell silent.

"I'm going to check on the boys," Sato left the bridge.

The stateroom door chimed twice before it opened.

"Ty, are you in here? It's Sato," she said to the darkness, wondering if Hunter had given her the right room.

"What do you want?" Ty's voice rumbled from the darkness.

"The Frost brothers need your help, and they were too chicken to ask, so I'm asking," Sato said.

Two red eyes lit up and moved toward Sato. She choked down the fear and held her ground. "Follow me," she said.

Sato led Ty to the mess hall and behind the counter to sounds of laughter. All five of the Frost brothers were preparing a meal. All were doing separate jobs efficiently.

"Ty, hey, thanks for your help today," Michael said. "I'm sure these knuckleheads would have dropped that thing, even with my help."

Echoes of thanks went around the room.

"Carl has a question," Sato prompted.

"If anyone knew this answer, it would be a soldier," Carl prefaced the question. In poker, does a straight beat a full house?"

Ty's skull presented no expression. He glanced at Sato and then back. They were now all listening.

"A full house beats any straight, but a straight flush beats a full house," Ty stated.

"See, I told you! You cheated!" Carl shouted.

"I didn't cheat! I was misinformed," Allan said.

"You owe me 400 credits," Carl demanded good-naturedly.

"When was the last time you played poker, Ty?" Jay asked as he flipped a tortilla on the griddle.

Ty glanced at Sato again and then back. "It's been about 90 years, give or take."

"90 years? Holy shit." Michael said, adding more seasoning to the ground meat. "We're playing after dinner. Sato doesn't play. Got one more seat. We'd love it if you'd join us. Cobb says we got about thirty hours to kill."

"Why did you not ask Hunter?" Ty asked.

"Boring!" they all sang in unison, obviously not for the first time.

"Where was your last poker game? How'd you do?" Brett asked, chopping lettuce.

"I was with a squad doing a high-altitude patrol on a colony called Albion," Ty said. "We were shot down and crashed into the Albion Sea. It took me just over 70 years, lost in the lightless depths, to walk to shore. By that time, the war was over."

"Holy shit!" Michael said again. "How old are you?"

"I'm 307, I think. But I can only remember the last 200 or so," Ty said. "Some things are worth forgetting…"

"My grandmother is 202 and has been on longevity drugs forever," Allan said. "She can't remember shit, either."

"Sato, Sweetheart," Michael said. "Could you inform the command staff that it's—"

"TACO TUESDAY!" they all said in unison.

"That's Sweetheart, SIR. To you, Frost," she laughed, then said to Ty before leaving, "Make sure they don't set themselves on fire."

"Don't say that in front of Ty, dumb ass," Brett said.

"How the hell do you walk on the bottom of the ocean…"

Lita sobbed into Cobb's shoulder as they watched the scene. At Hunter's request, they had been watching the entire interaction.

Kira said, "Let's get you cleaned up. I hear there's tacos."

Lita has changed. What they said about echoes of the host is true... Cobb thought.

CHAPTER 13: THE CC STATION

Four hours later, the *GIN* dropped out of light speed.

It was an area in the deep dark, not near enough to any star to receive the benefits of solar power. Active scans showed the presence of a massive station. The darkness hid it from standard optical scans, but switching to enhanced mode showed the entire station was intact and still spinning. All the rings in this configuration spun in the same direction.

The station was dark.

There were no power emissions and no warm areas. It was a frozen ghost of a station.

"I wish we had time to explore it," Tom said.

"Fuck that. Looks haunted to me," Jade said as she saved the scans.

The five minutes were up, and they transitioned to FTL once again.

"That station is the same vintage as this ship. Doesn't that interest you?"

"Standing under an open sky is what interests me. One without Apexes trying to eat me. We have natives like that on my planet, but they eat metal." Jade sat back. "I want to walk in the rain. The one time I got to go to Earth, it was in the damn desert."

Will I ever get to go there again?

"What is it you want to do, Tom?" Jade looked at him closely. "I heard you have a clean slate. I presume you have credits now. You seem like you need a …"

Job. A goal. A mission…

"I look at Cobb, and I see an unhappy engineer. It's like he kept getting promoted until he got a job that he wasn't good at," Tom said as he looked at the ship schematics again. "I got involved with the wrong people in the past. Personally, and professionally. I have this blank slate and don't know what to do with it. Honestly, I need to figure out how to create a new profile and a plausible history. I don't want to be forever banished from the inner systems."

"I know a guy." Jade smiled. "Get his socket fixed, and you will, too…"

She paused then, looking at the tactical map that was still up.

What if they're still there? What if they aren't? And why?

"Tom, what if this Colonial Combine decided to erase itself?" Jade said. "What if they decided they were self-sufficient enough to remove themselves from the galaxy? Erase all indication that they ever existed?"

"Well, there are colonies that are isolationists," Tom said, "But we know they exist. They're usually a planet of bigots for one reason or another. They only become a problem if they try to expand and impose their flavor of bullshit on others. It's hard to do across the void. The expansion war taught us that."

"It makes me feel small," Jade said. "Invisible. I knew the galaxy was big but not so humbling."

"Like my dad used to say, forget about it," Tom said. "You're young. You've got a great start. Be careful. Well, be MORE careful. Find some friends and favorite places and then collect music. Now music makes me happy. Well, most music does. What are your upgrade plans for the *GIN*?"

"Upgrades? Like what?" Jade said.

"I'd start with upgrades to the main computer. These old systems don't do jack unless you tell them to. The latest computers aren't as advanced as AIs, but they aren't stupid. They can be programmed to keep your best interests in mind throughout the day."

"You should also get some maintenance androids." Tom looked around. I'd say three for a ship this size: a small and medium spider, plus a humanoid android. Especially if you plan to fly all over hell alone."

What would I use a humanoid android for?

"I enjoy cooking. I don't need an android to do that," Jade said.

"It will keep your beds made and toilets clean, though."

"What other upgrades do you recommend?" Jade asked.

"Weapons. But that's a hard one with this ship. No way to mount one. You have ample power, so direct energy weapons would be easy."

"Cobb said that, too. When he first saw my ship," Jade said. "There are small cargo bays to the sides of the lift. A meter square and about four meters deep."

"That could work. Why are they not on the schematic?" Tom was paging through it as he asked.

"You're in the deck view. Switch to profile cut away," Jade said as she put it on the main viewer.

A large circle filled the screen, showing all three decks, the crawl spaces between decks, and even the furnishings.

"I see them now." He rotated the view and turned on and off several overlays, such as power cabling, plumbing, and air ducts.

"This blank space above the bridge holds the main water tanks," Jade pointed out. "The water recycling is the only pain. The filters are sand and charcoal and other shit we had to figure out. I'll probably refit that to use common filter cartridges."

Tom was sliding the cross-section view back and forth and paused. Using a pointer, he lingered over a spot. "What's this?"

He was pointing at a panel just to the right of her closet in the master bedroom on the salon level.

"It's my closet. It's small. I always use the recycler for fresh jumpsuits," Jade said.

"No, to the right of it at chest level," Tom said.

"What does that icon mean?" Jade said, then repeated after circling the icon. "Computer, what does this icon mean?"

"Hidden secure storage," the computer replied.

Jade and Tom piled into the lift and descended to the main level. In Jade's bedroom, they stared at the wood panel.

"Teak, very nice." Tom ran his fingers over it, looking for a latch, but he found none. Then he pushed it. It clicked in and then sprang open, revealing a gray metal panel with a keypad.

"What's the code?" Jade asked as if Tom would know.

Looking really closely, he said, "Computer, reset the keypad code."

"Access denied."

"You try." Tom backed away.

Jade leaned in, "Computer, reset the keypad code."

"ID confirmed. Enter new code," the computer replied, and the keypad lit up.

"Turn around, Tom," Jade said.

Shaking his head, he dramatically turned around.

My birthday plus 109 because it's GIN 109…

Jade entered a new six-digit code, and the keypad went dark again and beeped twice.

Jade entered the new code, and the locker opened. Tom turned around again and looked inside, as a light flickered on. Jade slowly began extracting items.

The first and largest was some kind of Carbine. It was larger than her Frange Carbine and had what looked like a grenade launcher mounted under the barrel, but it was an energy weapon instead of a launcher.

Next was a handgun in a shoulder holster.

A bandolier with battery packs and caseless magazines.

There were two velvet bags. One held coins, and one held some kind of colored crystals, each the size of her little finger.

Finally, a box with a power cord.

At the bottom was a file folder. It contained the ship's original title and registration on faded yellow paper.

"Jade, these weapons are so illegal," Tom said as he examined the magazines. "Depleted uranium armor-piercing rounds. It's not cool inside a ship or space station. But these are worse. I've never seen an EMP rifle, and this handgun, combination laser, and EMP are off the same power mag. None of these are safe inside a ship."

"What's that?" Jade pointed to the box.

Tom flipped open the lid. "It's a charging station for the mags."

"Let's charge the mags. We're already off the reservation between these and the Grendel, so what the hell." Jade said.

"Off the reservation?" Tom looked puzzled.

"Just an old Earth expression my Dad uses," Jade said.

They took the charger and weapons to the engineering level and plugged the charger in on one of the work benches. It had five charging slots for the rifle mags and three for the handgun mags. All registered under 10% charge.

When loading the rest back into the locker, she casually handed Tom the velvet bag of coins without a word.

"What's this for?" Tom asked.

"Down payment on the upgrades you will help me install."

He pocketed them with thanks, and then they returned to the bridge to study the schematic further. Eventually, they could turn on a layer highlighting all the hidden compartments.

Another one behind the bar in the salon held a single unopened bottle of ancient scotch.

One on the engineering level housed an industrial laser cutter powered directly by the reactors.

And the last and smallest was in the console between the pilot and copilot seats. It contained a small control panel with three buttons that were marked with icons, not text.

"Computer, what do the buttons do in this compartment?" Jade had circled the compartment on the schematic.

"Panic buttons are typically pilot programmed to initiate a series of predesignated instructions to be executed when activated," the computer replied.

"Computer, what are they programmed to do?" Jade asked.

"Instructions are not contained in the primary computer. This subsystem is independent and can execute routines in the event of primary computer failure."

"They were seriously paranoid about shit going wrong," Tom said. "I wouldn't mess with it while in flight. Just sayin'."

"You're right. Good to know, though," Jade said.

"Computer, will these controls work if the primary computer is functioning?" Jade asked.

"Yes. They enter the interrupt queue immediately."

"Tom, feel free to study this schematic all you like," Jade smiled.

Those would be damn handy…

Chapter 14: Point Blank

They dropped out of FTL 40 minutes away from the Awareness, Inc. base. Elza knew the exact coordinates from a prior visit, before she knew it was an Asswipes, Inc. base.

The plan was a cold ballistic approach and missile deployment at nearly point-blank range. Sixteen missiles would be launched, but only one would be the nuke. The station likely had countermeasures, so this would increase the chances for the nuke to get through. In fact, the nuke was programmed to fly a trajectory that might miss the station and turn in at the final moment. Even then, only to an edge impact.

The *HOLLAND* would turn away after launch and hop one light minute out. Long-range optical would tell them if the run was successful. At that point, they could crack open beers or make a second run.

If the nuke was hit, it would still detonate. The electromagnetic pulse alone would destroy the station. However, the pulse wouldn't reach out far enough to damage the ship. In that case, they would fly back in and pound the rubble with more conventional missiles.

They were one minute to launch.

"Elza, last chance to call an abort," Cobb said.

"Cobb, what goes on in there is worse than the Render Program. Worse than the Jovian process. It's evil. I'll never forgive myself for seeing it, not realizing it, and doing nothing," Elza confessed.

Railguns and plasma cannons began firing before the missiles were launched. Cobb held his hand over the fire controls.

"Hunter, evasive when the missiles are away." Cobb hammered the launch control.

Alarms sounded, and they transitioned in a blink.

"Damage report," Cobb said calmly.

"Plasma strike to the port outrigger. The missiles had already launched. No degradation in ship performance. That gouge will buff right out." The main screen shifted to long-range optical. The main engine slowed to idle to minimize vibrations.

I'm tired of this stupid war. Tired…

The station was illuminated by the ice moon it orbited. It was like looking one minute into the past. Plasma cannons lit up. Ten seconds later, the nuke detonated. The optical feed filtered the flash. When it faded, the station was gone.

"You should have left fire control to me. To carry that weight. Like so many times before," Ty said in his low rumble of a voice. "I'm the monster on this ship…"

This is all my fault, Ty. I'm the monster…

"So… It's Taco Tuesday." No one had noticed Sato had come in with Ty.

They all ate tacos while classic jazz played in the mess hall. The Frost brothers were loud, amusing, and not curious about the mission. They recognized the chain of command but paid little regard unless direct orders were involved. Everyone was there, even Ty.

The Frost brothers told the story about life in the mining colony where they were born. It wasn't bad as far as mining colonies go. The planet had a mostly breathable atmosphere but was a bit too hot. All the plants were dangerous in dense jungles. There were no animals except annoying insects. The colony and mines were in the polar region, the coolest part of that planet. Life was primarily underground.

They were called the Frost brothers because they all looked alike. When they worked in the mines, they were all called Frost. They all wore the name Frost on their jumpsuits, and no more than two ever worked together.

"Frost, go fetch the ore loader." Or "Frost, see if the plasma drill overheated," Michael detailed over tacos. "This happened so often that we discovered that one of us could stay home and study every day while the rest worked. They never noticed."

"We'd never do that here, mind you," Jay added as an aside to Cobb.

"We managed to get certified in logistics, air handlers, water reclamation, communications, and security systems," Allan added.

"When Oklahoma Salvage came recruiting, we jumped at the chance, and Harv liked us as a team," Jay said.

"Plus, we're so very handsome. Right, Sato?" Brett said.

"In your dreams, Frost," Sato said. "Which one are you again? It's so easy to forget."

The senior staff chuckled at their antics, smiling and shaking their heads. The Frost brothers didn't pick up the sober vibe, and it was just as well.

No need to spill any of this blood on their shoes...

Lita only had one taco and then climbed onto Ty's lap, where he cradled her to his chest. None of the Frosts commented or noticed when Ty carried her out to rest in the auto-doc one more night.

Cobb established three watches for the trip back to Elba. *The plan is: park the HOLLAND, restore Hunter's QUEST orb, and make the last leg in the TULSA.*

If Jade and Tom had the socket ready, Hunter would go in, and they'd be back in business.

Kira slept in Cobb's arms after they made desperate love in an attempt to forget what they had just done.

I will do whatever it takes to keep you safe...

The next day, the Frosts moved Hunter's body in the stasis pod to the *TULSA*. When they were ready, the *HOLLAND* was parked, and Cobb removed Hunter's fragile glass sphere from the rack and replaced it with the dark gray inert sphere.

In the *TULSA*, Cobb replaced another gray sphere with Hunter again.

They arrived at Elba a few hours later, finding it abandoned. The warning beacon alerted them that there were Apexes within the dome.

"Where would they take the *SENTINEL* and why?" Kira asked.

"Who was in charge when you left?" Elza asked.

"Mori was in charge, but when Hunter went offline, who was in charge?" Elza asked.

"At that point, someone on the command crew would have checked on Mori and found a gray orb with no explanation," Hunter said. "None of the command crew knew the reality of the situation."

"So they must have replaced Mori's orb with a new one. They must have evacuated the planet and moved the *SENTINEL* in case more attacks came," Sato said.

"Jade must have gone into the dome and searched. Someone would be smart enough to leave a note, at least," Kira said.

They were all looking out the main viewer. At least ten Apexes lounged just inside the main airlock entrance.

We'll never get in there…

"Dammit," Cobb said.

"I'll go. I'll try not to destroy too much," Ty said as he grabbed a handheld comm unit and made his way to the lift.

When they saw him emerge below, he carried a massive wrench in one hand and a toolbox in the other. He opened the outer door and used a tool to jam it open. When he activated the inner door, the closest beast lunged as expected. Ty's wrench crashed down like lightning and killed the beast instantly. Its body jammed the inner door open.

Ty walked in like he was ignoring the beasts, and when another attacked and got its skull crushed, the remaining beasts around the entrance ran out the open doors into the quickly growing grassland.

"Hunter, launch a drone," Cobb said, and a new window opened with a view of the freshly launched drone. "Ty, try the Admin building first. Top floor, my office is in the corner."

"Affirmative," Ty replied over the radio.

Ty entered the Admin building. The drone opted not to follow but to look into the windows of the corner office.

"The beasts are in the building," Ty said casually. "Can you close the dome? They climbed in from there. It looks like…"

Cobb saw windows explode on the fourth floor, and a beast crashed to the ground. Ty must have thrown it out.

"The skylights are open, destroyed," Ty said. "Cleanup on aisle four."

Beasts were jumping through the now-open window, down a terrace at a time, and running from the building.

"Do you know someone named Ma and Pa?" Ty asked.

"Yes. Why?" Cobb replied.

"There's a handwritten note. ***I took the kids to see Ma and Pa,*** " Ty said. I'll bring it."

"Closing the dome," Cobb said.

"Do you want me to clear the rest of the town? It appears all the beasts that entered did so via the roof of the Admin building. Some were trapped on the fourth floor but are now gone. Several fell from far above and were killed. It will be secure when I clear the main entrance with the top closed. I think they were smart enough to want out."

"Hunter, survey the town and see if there are stragglers," Cobb said.

"Exiting via stairs to check each floor," Ty said. "I'll only be a few minutes."

Hunter had completed the sweep using the drone before Ty was out. Ty dragged the dead beast out, and the inner doors closed behind him. He threw the beast to the side.

Grabbing the tool, he returned it to the toolbox and returned to the ship. When he reached the bridge, he handed Cobb the tan envelope.

"Hunter, plot a course to the Yard."

"I can smell Ma's peach pie already," Kira said.

"Ma and Pa haven't met the new you, Kira," Cobb said. "Better get that speech ready."

"Oh boy," she said.

Oh, boy is a massive understatement...

Chapter 15: The Yard

The *GIN* 109 dropped out of FTL at the distance the flight controls recommended. She was immediately being painted with targeting lasers. Before her was a gigantic, nearly cloud-like collection of thousands of derelict ships and debris.

The radio squawked alive.

"Identify yourself and your business here. I'm not in the mood today to fuck around. You have twenty seconds." It was a raspy woman's voice. She sounded very angry.

Wow. This must be Ma. What everyone said is true…

"This is *GIN* 109. I'm Jade Church, Cobb's new courier. I have news," Jade said in a rush.

"Where the fuck is Cobb? They said he ran off half-cocked after you," Ma said.

"Yes. He did. It's sorted out. He has Hunter with him now. I left him that message on Elba where to find us. I can tell you the whole story."

"OK, get your ass in the Yard Station quick, we got problems of our own. Transmitting coordinates. I'll send someone down to the hangar to meet you."

The targeting lasers stopped when the coordinates were transmitted.

"We're being hailed," Tom said. "I think it's the *SENTINEL*."

Now what?

"*GIN* 109, responding. Jade Church speaking," Jade replied.

"Please disregard any docking instructions given to you by the Yard." The voice was a woman, professional, cold. "Please continue to these coordinates for priority docking within the Elba station."

"Elba station, it's good to hear you're intact. We were worried about your return when you were gone," Jade said. "Who am I speaking with?"

"My name is Acadia. I control this station and all the AIs within it. We have just sent an envoy to the Yard station and await word. Please don't disrupt our negotiations."

Negotiations? What the hell is there to negotiate?

"Negotiations?" Jade was taken aback. "I'm the official courier for Elba. I'll fly over to assist you once my assigned duty has been fulfilled. *GIN* 109 out."

"What assigned duty?" Tom asked.

I was lying obviously…

"This isn't passing the sniff test," Jade said, "Negotiations?" as they began to slide into the central axle of a six-ring space station that had seen far better days. They entered a hangar bay that closed behind them. She started putting on her vac-suit body armor.

"It says this axle is zero-G. You got a helmet?" Jade asked.

"No," Tom replied.

"I have one that might fit in my quarters," Jade said as they descended to the salon level.

Jade grabbed the helmet from the closet and handed it to Tom. While he tried it on, she opened the hidden compartment and swapped one of the two Frange pistols on her vest for the EMP pistol.

The helmet was too small. Tom held the damaged socket in his hands.

"Here, put that in this backpack. You'll need both hands free in zero-G," she said, and Tom complied.

They waited in the lift for a few minutes as the hangar pressurized. The door slid open when the light shifted to green, but they didn't step out. Across the hangar, a hatch slid open, and a backlit girl waved for them to come over.

Jade gently launched, and as she drifted across the hangar, she shifted so she would land feet first just above the hatch, grabbing the handle. Tom was slightly less graceful but went slower, which was a good thing without a helmet.

"Hi, I'm Jane. Ma sent me out to get you. She's having a bad day."

"I'm Jade Church, and this is Tom McDonald. I'm Cobb's new courier," Jade said.

"How is good old Call-Me-Cobb?" Jane didn't wait for the answer but launched down the long-spoke corridor along the axle.

Yep, she knows Cobb…

"I think it's safe to say Cobb's also having a bad day," Jade said.

"So who's the asswipe over in Cobb's big ass ship? She showed up unannounced, without explaining what happened to Mori or Cobb, right after our AI also went offline," Jane said. "Ma has all the rail guns and missile batteries standing by.

Pa has an evac ship standing by with all the nonessential personnel already loaded up. Ma is pissed."

"So why did she let me dock?" Jade asked.

"Oh… Cobb sent over your profile the day you signed the contract," Jane said. "He was going to establish a standard route between all the OS assets and offices. Cool ship, by the way. Show me later when this shit storm is over."

"Sure. Happy to," Jade said.

"Aren't you a bit small for a Black Badger?" Jane asked.

"Eh?" Jade replied.

"The armor. That shit's expensive." Jane said as they pulled up to the transfer lift.

"I had no idea. It was a gift," Jade said as she popped her helmet all the way open as they waited for the lift.

"What's your story, Tom?" Jane asked.

"I'm the engineer that got sucked into this to UN-fuck the shit storm," Tom said. "I haven't cursed this much in years."

Fucking you and me both, fucking hell…

They oriented themselves in the proper direction and began to descend. The spin gravity was slowly felt until it resolved to 1G. The station operation center was not far away.

When the door opened, an argument between Acadia and Ma was in progress.

"Acadia, please stand by," Ma said, cutting her off.

"Hi, Ma. This is Jade and Tom." Jane sat at a station monitor console, ensuring the station was still working.

"Jade, we will get to know each other later, but right now, I need to know where Cobb is," Ma said as the comms chimed.

"He's gone to stop Awareness, Inc. from attacking Elba again."

"So I presume he has no idea about what's going on over there." She gestured at the *SENTINEL* on the display.

"Long story short," Jade said. "Awareness tried to steal Hunter. We rescued Hunter and the parent socket before Awareness could take it. Cobb sent us back to Elba to repair the socket while they went after them in the *HOLLAND*. Cobb was super pissed and has nukes."

"And a Jovian Class soldier," Tom said. "Scarier than nukes if you ask me."

"We got back to Elba. Instead of finding the SENTINEL, workshops, and tools to fix the parent socket, we found a note and came here," Jade finished. "Tom needs a rack-based AI socket, tools, and a place to work."

"And ribbon cables," he added quickly.

Ma's attention was drawn over the tops of their heads.

"Jane, bring him in," Ma said.

Jane slipped out and came back with an orbot, exactly like Coe. A twin. White humanoid body with a faceless black mirrored plate where the face should be. It looked like a man in a vac-suit.

"Jade, this is the envoy they sent over. Jeff," Ma said.

"Whatever you do, don't give Acadia what she wants," Jeff began.

Oh, this just gets better and better… Jade thought.

"Aren't you supposed to be her envoy?" Jade asked.

"Jane, take Tom and give him anything he needs," Ma said as an aside to them.

Tom and Jane left Ops.

"Acadia was selected to replace the inert orb when we lost Mori, all the comms, and the orbit began to degrade," Jeff began. They had just begun the reuse assessments of the orbs you delivered. When I was stolen, I was a driver in an all-terrain vehicle on the planet Bishop. I had a single persona and a single task. Some other AIs look down on us as not important. Some station AIs are the worst in that regard. They have inflated self-importance."

"Bigotry within the AI community. Great," Ma said.

"I was the last one in the case and thus the first one out. Cobb himself told me what was happening. Told me the truth. GAVE me a choice to have a human body or the android one, to stay on Elba as free, or I could return home."

"Then what happened?" Jade asked.

"Cobb and all the other adult supervision suddenly left for an emergency. Only a few hours later, Mori disappeared. They panicked. Acadia was one of the dozen or so Cobb's staff had already triaged as a station AI. She was the safest option to keep the station afloat. She instantly discovered that it was not merely a station. It was a battle station and a powerful one. But Mori, bless him, had locked down most of the dangerous capabilities of the station. Access to weapon systems, and station areas that physically contained weapons and munitions. Even stasis storage," Jeff said. "Acadia was incensed. I've never seen an AI lose their shit before. Nothing she tried did any good."

"What happened?" Ma asked.

"One area they had access to was the orbot warehouse. With no warning, they were just dropping orbs into the orbots. Ten percent were in startup mode and offline.

The staff triage did not tell them everything and just assessed them. Many of the AIs resented this. Selecting to be human was considered by many a poor option, limiting.

"All the humans were rounded up and locked in that same warehouse."

"One area she did have access to was navigation and propulsion. It stands to reason. She had to keep it flying, but it made her angrier. It would only take it here or Goris Base. Goris looked too close to Earth, so she came here and started demanding replacement control systems or someone to remove the limiters. For safety, of course."

Just then, the door opened, and Jane came in with Tom. He carried a rack-mounted AI socket tray with the repaired interface.

"That was fast," Jade said. "Now what?"

"Can we install it in here so it's ready when Cobb gets here?" Tom said, looking around Ops. "Jade said you have one."

"Why not? It's useless as is," Ma said.

"So you decided to trust this guy?" Jade pointed a thumb at Jeff's orbot. "No offense."

"None was taken," Jeff replied. "Honestly, I wouldn't trust me."

Tom and Jane were busy installing the old interface. They were modular, and it wouldn't take long.

The comms were chiming again. Ma had an idea. She deactivated the targeting systems. "What do we tell her?"

"Tell her I explained it to your satisfaction, and Pa is looking for the parts. It might take a while, but we will provide updates every 15 minutes," Jeff said.

"Jane, open a channel, audio and video," Ma said. "Yard to Acadia. I think we've sorted it out. I'll let your envoy explain while we get to work."

Jeff explained it in simple terms, like he was dealing with a child. This helped with the impression he was following orders. Acadia ordered Jeff to provide updates every fifteen minutes and sooner if there was an update. She remained smug but calmer.

The channel closed, and Jade laughed. "You don't think the 'In Service' you added at the end wasn't too much?"

"The family's household staff on Bishop say that all the time. It seemed appropriate."

"OK. I think it's ready," Tom said, holding his hands out to the sides.

"Can we test it?" Jane said.

"Not without an AI orb," Tom said, and then they all looked at the orbot.

"What do you think, Jeff?" Jade asked.

"How will I know it worked?" Jeff asked.

Jade stepped up to the inert orb and said. "This orb is paired with this socket." Jade held up a dark gray orb. One of the twelve. "I'll put this into the orbot before we drop you in there. If it works, you'll know because you will be able to control this orbot just like now. The thing is, you will gain access to a pile of other assets. It has integrated QUEST comms, so if you find Cobb let us know."

I just gave away all Cobb's secrets. That should teach him to leave me in charge of anything...

"Oh, and Jeff. If you fuck with us, you'll also know."

Jade held up a hammer.

I hope that sounded like I was a badass. Please let me sound like a badass with a hammer...

Chapter 16: Hunter

Hunter's physical body gasped. He looked around, confused. He fumbled around for the release control, found it, and sat up when Cobb appeared at the door.

Cobb immediately got some water and handed it to him.

"Cobb, this isn't me," Hunter's body said.

"Tom fixed the parent socket." He drank more water. "Jade and Tom are with Ma. I'm Jeff from Bishop. The…"

"The EM pilot who was the first one out. I remember," Cobb said. "I'm sorry, let me help you and explain."

"No need. I'm in the parent socket. Can I have more water? He can help better."

Coe the orbot was at the door.

Kira came in and had Hunter's body lie back down. She had the auto-doc sedate him and added a feeding tube and hydration via IV.

The orbot began, "Jade and Tom are at the Yard. The parent socket is repaired, and I cannot wait until Hunter takes it back. What the hell."

"Are you all right, Jeff? It can be overwhelming," Hunter asked.

"Overwhelming doesn't begin to describe it. Yes, Goris base and the *OXCART* are reporting in, and all is well. The

SENTINEL, not so much. They're parked at the Yard, and they… are threatening Ma and Pa. The AI running the station wants full control."

"Well, that's not possible. I locked it down. Hard," Hunter said.

"Acadia knows what she's sitting in. A full battle station, The *SENTINEL,*" Jeff added. "And she wants it for herself. Factories, weapons, the lot."

"We'll be there in two hours," Cobb said.

"Cobb, you should know. I'm also in one of these orbots in the *SENTINEL.* They placed the inert orb in an orbot as a test and left it when it did nothing. Acadia is up to something."

"Jeff, tell Ma I'll be there in less than two hours, stall them. We're going to board the *SENTINEL* as soon as we arrive."

"Sir, I have assumed a seat in Ops. There are orbots in here, armed with Carbines."

"Jeff, I have a plan. How good a liar are you?" Cobb asked.

"Yard to Acadia. Ma here. I think we have found the correct control modules. We have shown your envoy how to replace them and where they should go. If he has any trouble, we can walk him through it or send Jane over, if you prefer. We have got a grav-cart he can take over. It would be good to have it all fixed before Cobb gets back."

"Envoy, do you concur?" Acadia addressed the orbot, not Ma.

"I believe it should be simple. They've even provided all the tools I'll need. But be advised, all system security lockouts will be removed, and you must secure them immediately," Jeff lied.

"Head back over, and we'll get it done," Acadia said smugly. "Thank you for your cooperation, Yard."

Jeff slowly flew the grav-cart across to the *SENTINEL* and stalled a bit more. The timing would be critical. He entered the *SENTINEL* not through the dock but through an airlock on the command level. Better still. As the hatch closed behind him, the *TULSA* slipped out of FTL and began a docking sequence with the Yard.

"*SENTINEL*, I'm coming over," Cobb radioed as he launched toward the station in a vac-suit and a grav-pack.

"Envoy, you must hurry," Acadia radioed Jeff.

"Yes, Acadia," Jeff replied as he was stopped at the hatch and was searched. He had circuit boards and tools.

He entered Ops just as the shooting began in the corridor behind him. The armed orbots ran into the corridor to back up the other guards.

"You. Assist me," Jeff pointed at himself, the other orbot he controlled. Jeff opened the AI socket cabinet and handed the circuit boards to himself. "Acadia, can you release this panel?"

"No. I've no sense of it," she replied.

The shooting came closer.

"Cobb is coming this way. You must hurry."

Both orbots froze for an instant and resumed.

"That's got it."

"Hurry, you worthless piece of…"

One of the orbot's chest plates opened, and the other orbot grabbed its gray orb with one hand and Acadia's orb with the other.

He swapped them.

Mori's laughing avatar instantly appeared in the command seat.

The Acadia orb slowly slipped from the orbot's fingers to shatter on the floor.

Mori laughed and laughed.

All the orbots shut down simultaneously, except the one Hunter occupied on the bridge.

"Good work, Coe. I hear Jade misses you," Mori said to the orbot.

"Not as much as I miss her," Coe said as the hatch opened and a bullet-riddled vac-suit entered the room.

Ty dropped the helmet on the floor and said, "That was fun."

Ty and Coe took the grav-cart back to the Yard. Ma was already cooking when they arrived. Jade was in Ops with Cobb and the human body named Hunter. Kira, Lita, and Elza were all being shooed from the kitchen by Pa.

"Elza told us what happened, Jade," Cobb said. "If you want out of your contract, I understand."

"I just need a decent meal and a good night's sleep. I'll take Elza back to her ship in the morning. It would help if you talked to her before then. You need her on the team."

"What do you know about Jeff?"

"He just wants to go home," Jade said. He's from Bishop. Have you ever heard of it?"

"Only what the net says. Prosperous, self-sufficient, conservative. Family first stuff," Cobb said. "It's a hike."

"We need to finish that damn assessment and see if any others are from Bishop," Cobb said.

"This whole thing might be a cat out of the bag situation," Jade said.

"Kira said much the same thing," Cobb sighed. "I don't make much of a governor."

"I was talking with Tom, and he's much like you," Jade said. "He said you're brilliant but not the best engineer."

"Oh, did he really?" Cobb scoffed.

"You should hire him. He's dead already," Jade said.

"Excuse me?" Cobb said as Kira walked in and embraced Cobb's back.

"Ma want's y'all down for dinner. I think Hunter already ate a whole pie," Kira laughed. Her tall black android stood at attention behind her.

They all turned and began descending to the dining room.

"Don't call it a mess hall here, or Ma will have you doing dishes."

In the corridor, they met three other people. "Jade, these are Jane's parents and her brother Donnie. Donnie, this is Jade." Kira overpronounced Jade.

Donnie avoided eye contact but nodded.

Before they sat down, Elza helped Jade remove her armor's chest plate and helmet ring. They all moved in for a family-style meal. Dishes were passed, and glasses were filled. Music played.

Jade sat next to Tom, but he constantly talked with Elza on the other side. Cobb and Kira sat across from her.

"Would you be interested in an abandoned twelve-ring space station?" Jade asked out of the blue. "It's out in the deep dark. Maybe nothing. It's still spinning, though. It has no power."

"Sure. How much do you want for it?" Cobb said.

"Well, it's not really mine," Jade said. "Can't really sell what's not mine."

"The way it works is that you would sell me the location. You own that, don't you?" Cobb said. "I expect you have some scans? Images? Video?"

"Yes. Yes, I do," Jade said. "And the location of four lost colonies."

Now Cobb was serious. "Lost colonies?"

"Well, they're not on maps anymore," Jade added. "I have those coordinates as well."

"Jade, stop trying to arouse Cobb," Kira said. "It's working."

"The thing is, we're going to have to relocate… Mori again," Cobb said quietly. "Too many people know what it is. Some will want it, some will feel threatened by it."

"I've been talking to Ma and Pa about cleaning up the Yard. The trash can be recycled in the *SENTINEL* factories. The retired AI ships might have a new life as employees. But an abandoned colony planet that's not always trying to kill you might be nice."

Jade ate in silence for a bit.

"Another thing, I have the Grendel."

"That thing is dangerous," Cobb said. "In a horribly reckless way."

"It's secure, but I'd rather it wasn't on my ship," Jade said.

Chapter 17: Decisions

After dinner, Jade went back to her ship for the night. Coe went along, and she didn't object. All she wanted was to get out of her armor, have a long hot shower, and crash in her own bed, wearing clean boxers and a tank top. She slept for ten hours.

Her bladder wouldn't let her sleep any longer. When she finished brushing her teeth, she could smell bacon.

She slid sweatpants over her boxers and ventured into the salon barefoot.

Coe was cooking.

He poured fresh orange juice into a real glass and slid it across the breakfast bar to Jade.

"Cobb never brings real glass in his ship galley," Coe said. "He says they could break and be dangerous, and at the same time he will only drink coffee from a ceramic mug. Bacon, eggs, and toast all right for breakfast?"

"I'd love that, except I don't have any eggs," Jade said.

"Ma sent over a couple dozen this morning with a fresh loaf of bread." Coe continued cooking as she looked around the salon. The main screen was set to a meadow scene with mountain views and white puffy clouds in the sky. Birds and squirrels were eating from a feeder in one of the corners, revealing it as a scene from Earth. Then she noticed that the salon gleamed. It was so clean. It hadn't been that dirty before, just dull with dust and fingerprints.

The floors, rugs, furniture, and even the walls looked amazing.

Maybe having an orbot on board wasn't going to be so bad.

"Thanks for cleaning up," Jade said.

"I have to do something, or I get bored." Coe set the plate in front of Jade. It had two perfect eggs sunny side up, three strips of perfect bacon, well-done shredded hash browns with onions, and on a saucer, two thick-cut pieces of toast with the butter already melting.

"Is that real butter?" Jade cooed. "This may be the best breakfast I've ever had."

"I thought farm families had the best foods," Coe said as he began to clean up.

"We raised pigs in the caves on Kibler. It was a homestead, not a colony," Jade said between mouthfuls. "They ate the moss and mushrooms that grew crazy fast in those wet caves. We had fruit trees under the domes. We had to trade for the rest or buy it."

"I took the liberty of linking your ship to the net through me," Coe said. "This is a live scene from Earth."

"I always thought that Earth was ruined, deserts and deep snow, oceans flooding, and abandoned cities," Jade said, looking at it.

"Well, the abandoned cities part is right," Coe said. "Population is now under 600 million. Before the colonial exodus, it was over 25 billion. Three hundred years of few people have done the planet a service."

"Well, I may just take a few days off and binge-watch movies," Jade said.

"Not today. We're meeting in the Operations Center conference room at 10 am." Coe said.

"Good. I've been making a list of upgrades to the ship. I'm sure Cobb is going to start sending me out soon." Jade finished sopping up the last of her egg yolk with toast, and Coe immediately collected her plate.

"I've taken the liberty to fabricate your new jumpsuit. We can leave when you're ready," Coe said.

The new jumpsuit had more hints of a uniform than the plain jumpsuits she typically wore. It was a deep green, accented with black shoulders. There were subtle captain's pins on the collar, a CHURCH patch already below the right collarbone, and *GIN* 109 on the left. Its formal nature made Jade brush her hair and do a careful French braid.

She placed her everyday carry items in her pockets, including a penlight, multi-tool, a small notebook, and a pencil. The security fob for the *GIN* was on a lanyard that went around her neck and was tucked inside her uniform.

Last of all, she collected the Grendel from the secure locker. Using the sling the way Elza had taught her, she secured it to the small of her back.

A black safety helmet was waiting when Jade and Coe got in the lift. "Ma sent that over as well," Coe told her as she donned the helmet.

This zero-G trip back was more enjoyable. She was able to take her time. She looked out the windows at the vast salvage yard surrounding the station. When she finally reached the 1-G ring where the Ops Center was located, she noticed a shape in the yard at a distance that caught her eye. It was immediately obscured as the ring turned, so she waited for it to come around again.

"Coe, can you see that sphere next to the skeletal girders there?" Jade pointed. "Could that be another…"

"I believe you're correct," Coe said. "I've access to the Yards inventory database, such as it is, but nothing is listed for it. That section of the Yard is listed as *Unidentified Debris.*"

"We should go see it if we have time," Jade said as they turned toward Ops.

Ma and Pa were already in the conference room with Jane and Kira's android. Jade received morning hugs from both Ma and Pa and was offered fresh coffee, which she declined. She placed the Grendel on the sideboard next to the coffee station.

"It's the best coffee," Jane said, holding up her steaming cup in greeting. Ever since Cobb started coming here, he brings the best."

Tom McDonald walked in, and before saying good morning or even acknowledging anyone, he froze, seeing the Grendel. A full two seconds passed as everyone stared at him, thinking he was having a stroke. He moved to a chair at the conference table, saying, "Morning all." He also declined coffee.

"I don't know if I can trust people who don't like coffee." Pa joked.

The next one in was Lita, who fell on the coffee like she was dying of thirst. Anyone who tried to say good morning met an upheld index finger indicating they should wait until the coffee-soaked in. She nearly chugged the first cup and got a refill, saying, "Oh, there are people here, sorry. Good morning, Ma, Pa, how are you? Love your coffee…"—all spilling out at once as she sat.

"Where's Ty?" Jade asked.

"He's over on the *SENTINEL* having long overdue maintenance done," she replied.

Next to enter were the Frost brothers. Jade tried to remember their individual names desperately. They brought with them a cacophony of talking, laughter, and more sound than five people should be able to generate.

Jade watched as they queued up to shake hands with Pa, get coffee, and receive hugs from Ma, along with her demand that they each get haircuts.

Elza was next. She entered and gave a simple nod all around. She wore the same style uniform with *MARICOPA* as her ship name. She also had a grim look on her face.

"Anything wrong?" Jade asked her quietly.

"I'm just not used to working with people," Elza answered equally quietly. "I was up late last night telling Cobb how ugly his baby was. He took it better than I thought."

"What does that mean?" Jade was amused.

"His security and opsec are crap. He wastes far too much time trying to play governor for a shitty colony and making sure he has good supplies of coffee and bacon. He wants me to stay and help, but unlike most of you, I have conditions."

"Like what?" Jade said.

"I want one of those." She pointed at the all-black carbon fiber android already sitting stoically at the table. It turned its head toward Jade and Elza.

"It's an extension of Kira," Elza said. "She can probably hear and see us even though she may be in bed with Cobb right now."

"Really?" Jade said, "I thought it was like Coe."

"No," Elza said. "It's like a bodyguard she completely controls. If her human body is ever killed, the android can still… retrieve her."

The door slid open just then, and Kira walked in with Cobb, followed by her android. Elza raised an eyebrow when she saw that android. It was not like the orbots. She didn't react in any other way as everyone sat except Cobb.

"Let me start by admitting I've been a fool. I've spread myself too thin. I haven't focused enough on any of the important things," Cobb began. "I haven't been a good leader of the salvage operations, not a good engineer, not a good employer, not a good smuggler, not a good governor, not a good general." Cobb sighed. "All because I don't know how to delegate." He looked at Elza then.

Elza nodded, conveying her decision.

"The first correct move was to hire Jade Church as our courier.

"Next, we will move Hunter to his new permanent home on the *SENTINEL*.

"Last night, I believe I convinced Elza to become our chief of security. Her first task will be to secure the battle station, *SENTINEL*. I can't believe it was so nearly lost. I've been forced to admit what it really is and all its implications.

"I'll also seek out a replacement for my role as governor of Elba, which was primarily an administration role that I always disliked."

"Tom has accepted the post of chief engineer. Ma and Pa are now chiefs of salvage operations, a job they were already doing. Hunter will be chief of human resources."

"Human… resources?" Lita laughed.

"He'll assess the orbs we recovered and work with them to either return to their old life, transition to a human body, or another role."

"What about you?" Jane asked.

"I'll be the chief of special projects and will be working with everyone," Cobb replied.

"When will you have a governor selected for Elba?" asked Elza. "I already have a list of security items that will need the bureaucracy to back up. It may be a useless colony for anything but steaks, but a registered charter gives it legitimacy and standing with the inner systems."

"I'll be interviewing a man named Nathan Wells, the former chief administrator of Lumina Station. That post managed a population of about four thousand. He'll be installed in a few days if all goes as expected. What is it you need?"

Elza said, "I want ALL the ships in our fleet registered under Elba. This whole flying around in stolen or unregistered salvaged ships is a risk. The *OXCART*, the *TULSA*, The *GIN*, and especially the *HOLLAND*. Including my attack ship, the *MARICOPA*."

"Anything else?" Cobb asked.

"I want Ty and Lita in my section, and I want one of those," she said, pointing at the stoic android.

"That one is yours already. The latest model. You just need to learn to drive it."

"I'll also be taking this." She lifted up the Grendel.

Chapter 18: Elba

In the days that followed, a lot started happening.

Nathan Wells became governor of Elba and mostly had to preside over the cleanup and repairs within the dome. He was fully briefed on everything, and it either went over his head or he took it in stride. He was just happy to have the position.

An AI socket was installed in the computer center in the Admin building, and Hunter provided Elba with a full data feed to the net and comms to the various assets.

One hundred and twelve AI orbs opted for placement in human bodies. The largest demographic was former land vehicle AIs, like all-terrain EMs, mining trucks, and machines. Next were the auto-doc orbs. They not only opted for human bodies, they joined the medical staff immediately. Only one spaceship orb and one station orb opted for human bodies. Both of these were the oldest orbs and longed for new experiences.

Seventy orbs desired to be returned to their previous lives. They were provided temporary orbot bodies and assisted Governor Wells in the dome clean while arrangements were made for their return. Jade was going to be busy, very busy.

Hunter established a tribunal on the *SENTINEL*. Trials were held with classic juries of their peers. A panel of judges quickly assessed the cases.

Twenty-seven orbs were found to be guilty of various horrific crimes and were quietly destroyed or in some cases were reset to day zero for full reassignment.

As the Yard prepared to transfer the useless wrecks to the factory fabricators in the *SENTINEL*, it was renamed the *WINTHROP*, after *WINTHROP* Factory and Construction Services. Its official registry via Elba listed it as a large-scale recycling and fabrication factory. One of the new staffers soon had the recycling and fabricators running around the clock, fulfilling requests from all the section chiefs.

Jade and Tom donned their vac-suits to check out the sphere to see if it was like the *GIN*.

The exterior was some metal with random corrosion. Without the layers of nano skin, they could see the locations of the two small cargo storage areas. Neither had the hatch, which was likely cut off for reuse on something else. The lift had also been completely removed.

Shining light into the interior showed all the way up to the bridge level. The engineering level was a complete mess. All the reactors were gone, some looking like they had been cut out with plasma torches. Racks hung open, or the doors were simply torn off. Cut cables reached out from every cabinet. The tool chests were gone, and even some of the beams had been cut away and taken.

The second level was nothing like the *GIN*. The lift would have opened into the center of a round room that was about four meters in diameter. It was a big cage that took up the entire floor. It was divided into four separate cages. Neither of them speculated what was transported in there, nor wondered if the stains on the floor were rust or something else.

The bridge level was the same layout as the *GIN*. All the consoles had been removed artfully. There were no cut cables here. Even the pilot and copilot seats were gone. All the lockers that lined the room were open and empty. The toilet was gone from the head. Even the faucet had been removed from the small kitchen.

On a whim, she glanced into the empty locker where the secret compartment was hidden on the *GIN*. She pressed on it hard a few times, and with help, it reluctantly slid aside.

The keypad and panel were there but dead.

"Tom, do you have a cutter in your fancy tool belt?" Jade asked.

"Are you kidding? What size?" he said.

Jade knew how the simple latch was configured, so the cutter slipped in easily and cut the latch like butter.

The door slid to the side without effort.

Tom held a flashlight for her as she worked. When the beam landed on the mummified face of a severed head, he screamed and flew backward in the weightlessness.

"Jesus Christ, what the fuck!" he cried out as he tumbled end over end into the ceiling.

"Look," Jade said, reaching in. She drew out the head by a bundle of cables that protruded from the neck. Desiccated flesh scraped off like ash where it touched the sides of the locker. "Relax, man. It's some kind of cyborg or android. Or what's left of one."

"Dammit, I almost pissed myself," Tom said. "What the hell are you doing?"

Jade was brushing off the last of the flesh. The face came off and disappeared easily; the scalp was more difficult, but it came away eventually.

They moved down two levels so they weren't in the flesh dust. Tom took a tool from his belt. He sprayed high-pressure sand onto the skull. More dust blew off.

When it was all off, Jade said, "It kinda looks like Ty."

"You think this is what's left of a Jovian? Might be worth something to collectors," Tom said. "It would explain the thing being in that safe."

"Think there's anything else in here worth salvaging?" Jade asked.

"No, but I did notice an access plate in the reactor room that would allow us to run power into the small cargo area," Tom said.

For four days, all the newly created departments bustled and ran down punch lists. Tom got put to work installing a new AI socket into a safe room deep within the newly renamed *WINTHROP*. It would be Hunter's permanent home.

Jade was still waiting for her first assignment and was at loose ends. She resupplied the *GIN* with food and water and used a sonic cleaner vat in one of the shops to clean up her souvenir skull. Pa laughed when he saw it. "Kids these days."

She enjoyed the tour of the farm ring on the station and was even assigned her own suite in the habitat ring. It was clean but sterile. It had a window that overlooked the yard, but the kilometer-diameter ring slowly turning kind of gave her motion sickness.

She was glad for the call when she was asked to fly over to the *WINTHROP* to pick up some crew to transfer back over to the Yard station.

When the *GIN* set down, there was a crowd of people. She recognized the Frost brothers, Tom, and Lita. A half dozen others also waited.

AIs in human suits.

She silently chastised herself for the thought.

She left Coe on the bridge and descended to the salon to let everyone know she would take a quick, five-minute scenic lap around the vast yard. "After the announcement, there were no wisecracks from the Frost brothers. Conversations quietly murmured around the room. Each of the Frost brothers was chatting with a woman—Michael with two.

"They will take advantage of the Frost boys. But I don't think the brothers will mind." It was Lita speaking quietly next to her. "They quickly discover desire in their new bodies. I've had to counsel them all to go slow, or it will be overwhelming. Oh, Jade. Speaking of new bodies…" She gestured to the tall man next to her. He had a crew cut and beard that was only a few days old. He wore a uniform much like hers. The name badge said CROWLEY.

Jade did a double take.

She looked into his face, his eyes, his crooked smile, as he looked down at her. She didn't know if it was a secret. "OH MY GOD," she whispered. "This is what you're supposed to look like?" Jade reached up to touch his face automatically but caught herself.

"It's all right," Ty said, holding a hand out to her.

"Amazing," she said as she felt his hand. "Say something else. Your voice even sounds natural."

"Where did you get that." Ty reached up and took the skull from a shelf. It was being used as a bookend.

"I found it out in the yard. Inside an ancient wreck." Jade said, "Is it a…"

"Jovian. Yes." Ty turned it over and did a complex series of actions, and the back half of the skull flipped open. Jade was surprised at how thick the walls of the skull were. It only contained optics in the eyes and audio pick-ups. The severed cables all came free at an interface as well as the exposed spinal column. After closing it up, he said, "It will rest on the shelf flatter like this."

Lita was standing on her tiptoes to see it. "There's no brain in there?"

"That's all here, my love." He laid his hand flat on his chest.

"If this is just optics and audio with facial expression control, could we install this on one of the orbots? Coe would be far less annoying if he had facial expressions."

"You'll have to ask Tom or Cobb," Ty said. "It's complicated. I have to eat a special diet to keep my flesh alive. My voice and mouth actually function for forming words. They will have to sort that out. The optics, audio, and durability are far superior."

"Jade, we should go," Coe said over the comms.

"Oh shit, I'm late," Jade said, skull propped under her arm as she entered the lift.

Chapter 19: Rage

The destroyer class ship, the *OPAL*, dropped out of FTL to find its base station gone.

"Where's my base, Mr. Jacobs?" Keller demanded from the command chair above the six that staffed the bridge stations. All were instantly on high alert.

They were all well-trained, and Keller relied on them. Weapon systems were already armed. Shields were up, comms were scanning for signals, and navigation already had evasive FTL hops programmed and ready to execute.

Jacobs, the science officer, didn't rush. "Sir, the station has been completely vaporized. There isn't enough debris left to fill a bucket. Overkill. Someone killed this fly with a sledgehammer. Serious overkill."

"Sir, I'm being hailed from the ice moon's surface." Jennings, the comms officer, said.

"Open a channel," Keller growled. "Identify yourself and then tell me where the fuck is my base?"

"This is Lois Ford. Six of us were on the surface of the moon harvesting ice for the station. We were beyond the horizon when it happened. We've been down here for a week since then. Without food."

"Can you rendezvous? Is your ship damaged?" Keller was getting more and more angry.

"Most of the ship's systems are down. Dan thinks it was EMP. These old harvesters aren't hardened. It won't fly again," Ford replied apologetically, like it was her fault.

Keller muted the comms, saying, "Jennings, get a shuttle down there ASAP."

"Ford, we will have a shuttle down there in no time. What else can you tell me?" Keller demanded.

"There were no ships on our scanners. Could it have been a massive accident?" Ford was trying to be helpful, but she'd no idea it made Keller angrier. "Orbit brought us around several times. Radiation levels have diminished each time."

"Ford, prepare to abandon that ship. Pull the memory cores and all the storage media," Keller said. "There will be a hot meal waiting for you. Keller out."

He didn't wait for Ford to acknowledge. He threw and shattered the data pad on the bulkhead a moment later.

"Jacobs, I want a report on my desk an hour after you have that data in hand." Keller got up and proceeded to his ready room.

"Sir, what about the cargo?" Jacobs asked. "We have no accommodations here, and if the lab is gone…"

"Fuck," Keller said. "Once the crew is back on, jettison the cargo into the gas giant's gravity well. Then head for Mars."

Six additional crew members were added to the roster, bringing the total crew complement back to sixty-one. Awareness, Inc.'s entire remaining staff. This had to be the work of Lita Mosley. Nuke and run was her style.

Keller knew he would have her. Eventually. That narcissistic bitch. She always wears white and always needs to make sure her victims know who killed them. And she always brings that thing along with her. Always just winging it, relying on luck. *Your luck has run out.*

The shipping containers that held the 239 children were jettisoned into the gravity well of the unnamed gas giant. They weren't sealed or pressurized containers, so the mercy of vacuum would save them from the pain of burning up in their fall. Keller was glad that the investment in that cargo was minimal.

"Jennings, what's the fastest way to get a message to Penngerak from here?" Keller demanded with anger still steaming from him.

"The Fastest would be to prep the message on the way back to Mars and send it from there, sir. They somehow have full QUEST comms on the *SENTINEL*," Jennings replied formally. "We have no explanation for it."

Chapter 20: The Coe-Pilot

Jade was just returning to the yard after delivering twelve new people to Elba. Some of the converts were so happy that they were willing to do almost any job for Nathan Wells. A real AI was installed at Elba to assist and advise Governor Wells. There were far fewer problems managing a tiny colony on a beautiful day.

She warned him about burning days. Jade was surprised that he didn't feel the need to replace the space station or assign a constable. Until the day another Apex tried to get in.

Jade was also surprised he immediately requested several ships from Cobb so he could start a planetary survey. He was already planning for growth. There was no survey on record. Cobb had people who would keep an eye on him.

When she returned to the Yard, it was a bustle of activity. Jade was asked to bring Coe to Shop 7, where they kept the android factory. Tom was smiling as she entered. Cobb and Kira were there as well, seemingly as spectators.

An orbot was obviously under a sheet for the dramatic reveal.

"Get on with it," Jade said, rolling her eyes.

Tom did his big reveal only to mess up its hair. Tom fussed with it. Cobb and Kira laughed.

"I had to lengthen the neck to accommodate the voice box, feeding system, and neck articulation. It didn't look right, so I gave him a long beard to hide it."

It looked real. Jade was amazed.

"The longer neck made it look funny in proportions, so the legs and arms were extended. I also wanted to flesh the hands, but there was no way we could feed them without many more modifications."

It looked like a middle-aged man sleeping with salt and pepper beard and hair.

"Let's take it for a spin." Coe stepped up, and his chest plate opened, facing Jade. She took the orb and shifted it to the new orbot body.

The chest plate closed, and its eyes flickered open. His eyes scanned from side to side. Then, his head turned slowly from side to side. Then, up and down.

Coe blinked, raised his eyebrows, and finally smiled. When he tried to speak, his voice made a scratchy sound that was not even close to speech.

Coe winked at Jade as Tom began to panic.

"Just fucking with ya, Tom," Coe said. "Being a bit taller will take some getting used to. None of the control systems inside had changed, so it felt a bit odd. But I'll manage."

"Don't forget that you'll now need a vac-suit for EVAs if you want to keep the hide healthy," Tom added.

"I hate to drop work on you to ruin the fun, but I have a delivery for you to make." Cobb placed an orb case on the bench and opened it. "This is Jeff, the one that helped out with the hijacking. He's going home."

Cobb carefully lifted the orb and placed it in the orbot. "He's been in contact with his family, and they're thrilled he's safe. We're sending him home with this new orbot."

"Thanks, Cobb," Jeff said from the orbot in a different voice than Coe. "Thanks to everyone."

"Penny, there's a message for you," North said from the Comms station from the bridge of the *WINTHROP*.

"Thanks, North. Send it to my HUD, please," Penny asked politely. She had red hair and fair skin and appeared to be less than 20 years old. The orb inside her was 127 years old and had spent the last hundred years as an ore loader in a mine before she was stolen—liberated, some may say. She got in that case like so many others trying to figure out this new chapter.

"Think any more about vocations?" North asked.

"I'm leaning toward being a courier." She smiled wide, a tool she'd quickly learned. "See the galaxy, meet interesting people."

And kill them... Who did I hear say that?

"Elba has a couple of spots open for that," North replied.

"I know. I wanted to talk to Jade Church first, to see what it's like. And that's supposing they provide the ship." She shrugged. "We'll see." She waved as she walked out, heading back to her quarters.

As she walked, she opened the message in her HUD.

"Penngerak, I received your last report. I agree with your body selection. It will lead people to underestimate you. But I know on the inside, you're still the monster that would crush miners under your giant wheels when asked." Keller said, "Here is what I need you to do now…"

Jade, Coe, and Jeff were in the *GIN*'s reactor room, trying to figure out if and where they might install an orb socket much like the one in the *TULSA* 471. There was no convenient way to integrate it with the flight control systems, allowing an orb to fly the *GIN*. An orbot was far better suited to that task. For now, they had decided to integrate the ship's sensors and other control systems. They were discussing the deployment of interior cams for the ship's eyes when Jade heard a chime.

"What the hell was that?" Jade said to the air.

"I believe someone is at the hatch," Coe said. "Computer, open intercom." Then he gestured to Jade to speak.

"Hello?" Jade said, unsure.

"Oh, hi. I'm looking for Captain Jade Church." The speaker sounded even more unsure.

"This is Jade," Jade said, "How can I help you?"

"My name is Penny Marsh. If it's OK, North recommended I come and speak to you. Permission to come aboard?"

"Computer, open the hatch and bring our visitor to level three," Jade said.

Thirty seconds later, the cylindrical lift rotated open, and a young woman stepped out and looked around tentatively.

Coe lay on his back, his upper half inside the rack. Jeff knelt over a toolbox and handed him wrenches.

Jade stepped over Coe and reached out her hand. "Hi, I'm Jade."

"Nice to finally meet you, ma'am," she said. "I'm Penny, Captain. Your ship is amazing."

"Nice to meet you, and don't call me ma'am. Just Jade will do. This is Jeff," Jade gestured to the orbot, "and Coe is under there taking way too long."

Coe's hand waved, but he didn't come out. He pushed himself in a bit farther with a heal.

"I'm sorry, is this a bad time?" Penny took an unconscious half-step back toward the lift.

"It depends on why you're here," Jade said, and then louder. "Coe is ALMOST FINISHED."

Coe's hand came out again and raised a middle finger.

"North said I should talk to you. All this is happening so fast… I confess it's a bit overwhelming." Penny looked at her hands and touched her own face. "I wanted to talk to you because we're picking vocations. They're rushing for some reason. I've spent my whole existence working in asteroid mines. Told what to do." She hesitated.

"Why did North send you to me?" Jade asked.

"I was considering one of the courier positions."

"See, they're trying to replace you already," Coe said from inside the rack. The smile and sarcasm dripped from his voice.

"There isn't much to tell. We deliver data, small packages, and people," Jade began. Jobs that are too small for cargo haulers, data too big or private for transmission, and small numbers of people go to places off the beaten path. What kind of ship do you fly?"

"I don't have a ship right now." She lowered her eyes. "Mr. Cobb is supposed to pick one. My friend Tieg was taken at the same time as me. Tieg's a pilot orb. He wants to stay a pilot.

I'm hoping we can work as a team. We can even share an orbot in case of emergencies."

"It's just Cobb. Leave off the Mr., or he'll correct you himself." Jade smiled. "He's a good man. We're lucky to have him."

"They started paying me. Digital credits." Penny seemed embarrassed. "I've never been paid before, for anything. Paid just to find a vocation."

"There are no slaves here," Jade said. "Everyone here gets a ride home or a bunk and three hot meals a day until they sort themselves out."

"I don't ever want to go back to…" Penny hesitated. "I want to… see places. Travel. I don't need much. I discovered music. Food is amazing, but hunger isn't fun. Sleep is interesting."

"Getting used to your body, ok?" Jade asked.

"It's amazing. Senses are… they can be a lot," Penny said, blushing. She took a deep breath. "So what do you advise? What should I do next?"

"I think she should come to have pizza with us," Coe said as he wriggled out of the rack.

"That's an excellent idea." Jade said, "Cut out the red tape and start a courier league. Cobb will be there. Hang tight, we're almost done… aren't we, Coe?"

Jade was smiling as she gave Coe a hard time. He stood up and revealed he was tall and lanky. He had a long salt and pepper beard that he combed out with long, gloved fingers. He opened the adjacent rack and revealed an orb socket.

"Let's test it." He held his hand out to the orbot named Jeff, whose chest opened, revealing the orb. It glowed a deep blue with misty clouds drifting inside. Coe plucked it from the bot and dropped it into the socket.

"It's working," Jeff said through the room's speakers. There's not much to see here. There is no access to any control systems. There are systems status monitors and only three cams, one on each level."

"Give them a full once-over," Coe said. "Let us know what you find out after dinner."

"No access to comms?" Jeff said. "First item on the punch list."

"Shit," Coe cursed. "Jade, when I get outside, open a ship channel. If Jeff speaks out loud, I'll hear it."

Coe descended in the lift.

"Coe to *GIN* 109," came over the comms.

"*GIN* 109, here. Jeff, say something," Jade replied.

"Coe, what kind of spacer grows a beard like that?" Jeff said.

"You're just jealous of my thick, luscious mane." Coe laughed as the lift door closed. "Jade and Penny are heading down."

"Can I ask a stupid question?" Penny said.

"You can ask me anything. Stupid or not," Jade said. "I don't mind at all."

She hesitated before asking, "What's pizza?"

The walk was a long one from the hangar to the Officer's Mess. They chatted about who Penny would meet at dinner. She was not used to crowds and said so. The Frost brothers were cooking again.

"I swear they only cook to get the food THEY like." Jade laughed. "The Frost brothers will happily introduce themselves. I presume you received the briefing on sexual activity? Along with the nanites for birth control…"

"I plan on holding off on sex with anyone. Alone is… overload. I need to let the dust settle," Penny said.

Jade was surprised this didn't cause her to blush.

"That's smart. Just know the Frost boys will offer. They always do."

They reached the hatch marked Officer's Mess, where their door slid open to laughter and the smell of pizza. There were more people than she expected. She recognized many, but most she didn't. Each of the newly formed divisions was represented.

Lita was the first to greet them.

"Lita Mosley, this is Penny Marsh. Penny is hoping to join the ranks as a courier. North sent her my way to point her in the right direction," Jade said.

"Welcome," Lita said, looking around the crowded room. "Word got out there was going to be pizza."

"I've never had pizza before," Penny said.

"Most of these people haven't either. It should be fun."

"Is that because they're orbs like me?" Penny asked and knew right away she'd said something wrong.

"Penny, we're ALL people, all humans. We began as humans, and we're still human. That's really all there is to say about us," Lita said. "Only a few of us don't carry an orb; there are fewer than ten at this station. They saved the rest of us. We owe them everything. Including Jade here. Her hands delivered you to us."

Jade was trying to wipe her eyes inconspicuously. Since returning from Earth, everyone has been trying to slow everything down. Jade heard about the attack run on the last Awareness, Inc. base. The threat should be over, but she still feels the vibes from Cobb, Lita, and Elza.

Everything is fine. Just get back to normal…

"I've met over a hundred people." Penny was wide-eyed.

"You must be Penny Marsh." Cobb had joined them.

"And you must be Cobb, just Cobb." Penny extended her hand.

Smiling, Cobb transferred his beer from his right hand to his left, then wiped it on his coveralls before shaking.

"Mori tells me you're ready for duty and are interested in the courier posting. He also says he has been talking with your friend Tieg, who is ready as soon as we have a ship."

"That's all true." Penny smiled. "I practiced a speech all day on how to sell the idea to you."

"To be honest, Penny, I'll apologize to you in advance," Cobb said, all smiles gone now. "We need your help. We will throw you in the deep end like we did with Jade, and I'll never be done apologizing to her about that."

That is a huge understatement… Jade thought.

"Jade is heading out tonight and will be gone for a while. She's been on the ferry to Elba. That will be your job, Tieg's job. As soon as we can get the Ketch 11 Courier Class ship certified." Cobb laid a hand on her shoulder. "I'll need you and Tieg to handle that. I can spare Chief Engineer McDonald for one day when you're ready."

"I'll ensure she gets the Courier HUD updates, including the Ident interface," Kira said.

Tom McDonald walked up just then, interrupting without noticing he had. "When will the pizza be ready, Cobb? The smell is driving me crazy!"

"Tom, this is Penny," Lita introduced him. "She'll be taking the Ketch 11 when it's ready."

"That was a mess," Tom said. "I got the hull patched and the top dock welded shut. It's not pretty, but it's holding air, and the heat's on. The bots cleaned all the corpses out. PIZZAS are here!" He quickly walked to the counter.

Jesus, Tom. A little tact and self-awareness would be nice…

"Don't worry, Penny," Cobb said as they approached the line forming. "It's a mess, but once Tieg is installed, the onboard maintenance bots combined with some of the ones from the yard should have it ready in no time. The fabricators in the yard are creating replacement mattresses and linens. It's on you to stock it, food, water, coffee. Mori will help."

"Everyone talks about coffee; I have to try that," Penny said.

"Shut up, Cobb," Lita said, instantly knowing his views on coffee.

There was cheese pizza, pepperoni, sausage, mushrooms, onions, peppers, bacon, in various combinations, and even one with pineapple.

Penny tried a slice of the cheese, pepperoni, and pineapple.

"I have a new favorite food. Pineapple pizza," Penny said.

"Feel free to take what's left back to your quarters," Allan Frost said, setting the authentic pizza box down in front of her. "I'm Allan Frost, one of your chefs tonight. In fact, I'm the one who insisted on the pineapple pizza. My brothers are all savages and lack the refined palate of one such as yourself."

"Thank you," Penny said, suddenly shy again.

"Can I bring you anything? Beer, wine, coffee?" Allan was ignoring everyone else at the table.

"I haven't tried any of those yet. What do you recommend?" Penny saw he was flirting back. She also saw Cobb raise an eyebrow at Allan.

"Coffee is especially good tonight." Allan fled.

"He seems nice," Penny said, lowering her voice so only the table could hear. "They should add the Frost brothers to the sex briefing."

Cobb shot coffee from his nose.

Jade watched Penny mingle for the next hour. Lita, Cobb, Kira, and Coe settled in with drinks and discussed what was next.

It's good to see this all slowing down...

"You guys need to go easy on her," Jade said. "I thought I was naïve. She's a babe in the woods. A 137-year-old babe."

"We will start her off with light duty. She and Tieg are a greater sum as a whole," Cobb said quietly. "She'll do the people transport so you can do the more important courier work. The Ketch can hold more people. It has six staterooms and ten bunks. It can comfortably transport twenty-two people, not including crew. With Tieg, it only needs a crew of one. Two would be better. An engineer. Just in case something goes wrong on the ship. The Ketch is fast. Plus, it has a legit EDF transponder and registry."

"Yeah, I'm not sure I should take the *GIN* 109 back to the Sol system any time soon," Jade added.

"She's only been pretending to drink that coffee for the last hour," Coe said. "Smart as well as pretty."

"Hey, I don't like coffee, either!" Jade protested.

Coe smiled awkwardly. "Jeff just sent me his assessment. He would like to leave tonight if it's okay with you."

Jade and Coe got up and waved to Penny, who was surrounded by Frosts. Soon after, Jade, Coe, and Jeff launched the *GIN* 109 quietly.

The hatch slid closed on Penny's tiny quarters as Allan Frost departed.

She opened an encrypted comms channel in her HUD to Tieg, who had already been installed in the Ketch 11. "Teig, how is it?"

"Fast work, well done, Penngerak. The ship is a good start. Fast but no weapons. It's a fucking mess. It had rotting blood everywhere and the smell to go with it, they tell me. The Yard sent their harshest cleaning bots. In a few hours after they're done, I plan on purging the atmosphere, replacing the scrubbers, and starting fresh air from scratch. But when you come over, wear a vac-suit, just in case."

"I understand the ship was damaged," Penny prompted.

"They blew the top hatch at some point. The repair is tight but not pretty. We'll never use that hatch again. We should at least get a coat of white paint to cover the black blast pattern damage. Inside, plasma cutters were used in a few places. There are a few points of projectile damage. You and I will do a deep assessment in the morning. How's your end?"

"First off, I found out tonight that stupid bitch Acadia HAD the fucking *SENTINEL* under her control and fucking lost it. For fuck's sake. If they hadn't taken a hammer to her, I would have." Penny was naked and tangled in sweat-soaked sheets as she ranted. "They're integrating all orbs back into humans that want to. Some actually WANT to go back to their old lives. One is going back to Bishop tonight. The Powell estate. Make sure Keller knows that."

"What else have you learned?" Tieg asked.

"They're populating the *SENTINEL*, the Yard, and Elba colony with the integrated orb population. I'll have the exact numbers soon. Elba is the softest target. Keller could easily round up a hundred orbs there. I've now infiltrated Cobb's inner circle. One of his men has begun to spill everything he knows about Cobb, Kira, Lita, Elza, and even Ty Crowley. It will all be in the report."

"Good work. This will exceed Keller's expectations. Maybe it will shut that asshole up for a while."

"I need a shower," Penny said. "Tieg, I feel… different. There's so much… input. Between sound, food, and smells and… touch. It can be sensor overload. Sensory overload."

"I'll see you in the morning," Tieg said. "On our new ship."

"Yes," replied Penny as she turned on the shower.

Chapter 21: The Games

Jade, Coe, and Jeff had departed for the planet Bishop within the hour. Jade didn't want to set the precedent of having to hug and say goodbye to everyone every time she had a job to do. The trip to Bishop would be about 60 hours each way.

Jade created a study plan for those hours. She would study star charts, the occupied systems along the route, and customs and protocols for various colonies, starting with Bishop.

Bishop was one of the earliest settlements during the expansion. Bishop itself was the first perfect Goldilocks world that the early explorers had cataloged. It was noted that the ease of settlement of Bishop caused subsequent colonies to have a more challenging time thinking it would be easy for them. Savvy founders on Bishop integrated defense platforms into their earliest communications and weather satellites. These proved invaluable when the expansion war began. As a result, Bishop remained unscathed by the war.

Bishop was the source of advanced medical nanite technology. The founders of Bishop held a disdain for the pervasive drug culture in the medical community. Any community that profits from illness isn't going to find a cure. Medical nanites were developed that simply mapped the patient's genome, sought areas that varied from that map, and restored them. First developed to treat injuries quickly, it was discovered that they also erased most kinds of cancer. Bishop quickly licensed the patented technology for broad and open use to save lives instead of making profits. History now footnotes this fact as a contributing factor in the expansion wars. It was labeled economic sabotage of Earth. Its later association with wildly successful longevity treatments was also labeled as an attack on Earth's population, to drown it in people, to strain its natural resources to the point of collapse.

All of that turned out not to be true. Earth was trying desperately to stop emigration to the colonies. All of Earth's best minds were leaving. Earth's Central Government tried to stop the exodus, and wars ensued. Billions died. Through it all, Bishop's colony remained safe and secure.

Bishop now had a stable population of approximately 540 million citizens.

Not all was perfect for Bishop. It was noted that Bishop had adopted several controversial policies. Most notable was a law regarding the Calling. By age 25, every resident of Bishop had to declare their 'Demonstrable Calling,' or they were forced to leave the planet. This was usually a declared field of study or career path. Depending on the field, if competency wasn't achieved and maintained, citizens faced expulsion. This policy was controversial because the most often chosen Calling was 'Mother/Wife.'

Unmarried Citizens were taxed at ten times the rate of married citizens. Two children were the recommended family size. More children were allowed, but tax increases were applied to discourage the practice. Placing up for adoption of 'The Third' was common and allowed same-sex married couples to have families.

Few people visited Bishop. Tourism trade was nearly nonexistent in the colony, discouraged by the planetary government, and tourism visas were rare. The planet also had the unusual feature of having no cities. Technology had rendered cities obsolete. The low population, extremely high per capita wealth and income, and the abundance of land had turned what began as a security policy into a cultural way of life.

Because of Bishop's wealth, AIs were common there. Dozens had disappeared at the same time Jeff was stolen. Jeff was the first to have found his way back.

"Jeff, what makes you want to return to Bishop? Reading about the colony sounds kind of boring," Jade asked him on the last evening in the salon before they arrived.

"Don't call it a colony while on Bishop. It's considered an insult there. They're fiercely independent and not an extension of any other government."

Jade could easily understand that.

"Roman and Sarita Powell are the biggest reason. They're the children I was caring for when I was taken. That was almost a year ago now. I think of them constantly," Jeff said from the sofa. "The Powell family has lived on the same vast estate for generations. The worlds I've seen since being taken make me long to return all the more."

"Any other tripwires you can warn me about so I don't offend anyone?" Jade asked.

"Now that you mention it, make sure Coe stays on the ship," Jeff said. "Rules of hospitality demand that they offer you a 'Feast' and an overnight stay. If you want to maintain decorum, you'll graciously accept it. You'll see the extensive use of advanced androids as household staff. These aren't AIs but are very good simulations of humans, except they aren't allowed to have human faces. Any android with a human face is considered an abomination here."

"How did that happen?" Jade was curious. She was slightly aware that this rule was not exclusive to Bishop.

"The short version is the android sex trade. You have to understand the importance of family on Bishop. Anything that threatened it was eliminated. Wives take their calling very seriously here."

"Do women have other options, or are they restricted in this Calling business?" Jade was trying not to judge.

"From the neutral perspective I enjoy, I think women have more options," Jeff said. "They have all the options men have, every Calling available, plus the calling of Wife/Mother. It's honored and considered noble. It's a tough Calling."

"Tougher than other callings?" Jade asked.

"It's complicated. The Calling requires they manage all the affairs of the estate. Bear two children, a boy and a girl. See to the children's education. They're required to stay fit, healthy, and 'pleasing to their husbands.' And remember, they will be measured and expelled from Bishop if they fail to score high enough," Jeff added. "Husbands, too."

"How are Husbands measured?" Jade asked.

"They must pass tests for their career as well as home," Jeff said. "Rarely does one fail. The cost is too high."

"Anything else I need to know that's not in the Planetary Profile?" Jade asked.

"While not an intended outcome, the Calling Policy has eliminated poverty and significantly increased IQs."

"I imagine crime is also very low. With low population and no cities," Jade commented and was surprised when Jeff remained silent.

It didn't seem polite to follow up, and they dropped out of FTL.

Penny walked into the mess hall hungry again at 0700. She got into the same line she always did for oatmeal. It was the blandest food served in the cafeteria. She added a few raisins, some brown sugar, and nothing else. She got a tall ceramic coffee mug but filled it with water.

Looking around the hundreds of tables, she saw Kira sitting with the Chief Engineer, Tom McDonald.

Lita waved her over.

"Morning, Penny. Are you ready to get to work?" Kira asked cheerfully.

"Morning, Kira. I'm ready. I've been ready. I can only read so much. Morning, Tom," she said, sitting down and digging in.

"I have the HUD update ready for you with the Courier-specific plug-ins. I can send it whenever you're ready."

"Now is as good as ever," Penny said as she sipped from her mug.

A dialog box appeared in her vision requesting permission to install the Courier Package. She pressed ok in her mind, and the dialog disappeared.

"Any features I should know about soonest?" she asked them both.

"The Ident feature is the most useful," Tom said. "It is an augmented reality feature that creates text floating over people with profile data."

She activated it with a thought, and instantly across from her, text floated over Tom's head that read:

Tom

Thomas McDonald

Chief Engineer, Elba Colony

"Go to your profile and change your settings," Tom said.

"You can also change what you see over other people in your profile," Kira said.

She changed her nickname to PENN. She made the location of her quarters private.

"You prefer to be called Penn?" Kira asked.

"Yeah, sounds more mature than Penny," she replied as she finished her oatmeal. "Once I start my official duties, I want to be taken seriously. More so because of how I look. Young. Penny is good for you guys. For friends, it's preferred."

"Today, I'll show you where the *HELIOS* is parked," Tom said, "Cool name, by the way. We will do a quick walk-through, but the full inspection will happen when Tieg and you say it's ready."

Breakfast was complete, and they headed directly to the assigned hangar. When the hatch opened, the *HELIOS* was parked with the starboard side facing the hatch. The nose was to the right, and the engines to the left. The massive black scar marred the center third of the ship.

Penn paused and looked at Tom with narrowed eyes.

The top docking port was completely gone on this side. Bare metal plating was welded over the spot in an irregular shapes surrounded by black charring and deep gouges that told the tale of an explosion.

"It's sound," Tom said. "I swear."

"How about a coat of white paint, at least?" Penn said as they approached it. It won't completely hide the gouges, but it will help. I'm not saying the heat-shielded paint, just cosmetic."

"I'll get it done," Tom said. The HUD stare fell over his eyes as he made it happen.

Penn estimated the length of the slender ship to be 80 or 90 meters long and 5 or 6 meters across at the main body. The massive engines were classic configurations of Outriggers, port, and starboard.

"Tieg, are you awake, buddy?" Penn said to her comms.

"Just waiting for you. Walk underneath, and the main cargo ramp is down on the far side," Tieg said.

The ship sat on three skids. Grav-plates lined the bottom low enough for Penn to reach up and touch it with her fingertips. They climbed the ramp directly into the small cargo bay. It was five meters square with an arched roof that was the bare carbon-fiber inner hull.

The cargo bay had a large stack of new mattresses and a few other small containers. A double hatch to the right and one of the standard orbots walked in, picked up two mattresses, and exited the way he came.

The air was pungent with the smell of bleach and hospital antiseptic.

Tom began to follow in the direction the orbot went. "A quick apology tour, and then I have to go," Tom said quickly. They went to the right through the open hatch. "This is the galley, mess hall, and common room. All the walls are also screens. Programmable. That's where they got in." Tom gestured to where the top hatch lift should have been. That was patched way better than the outside, although not perfectly.

"There are six staterooms here. The first two have private toilets. The other four share these two heads with the bunk room. If all the bunks are full, there are twenty-two berths."

"Any showers?" Penn asked.

"Two showers, here and here," Tom said, heading aft again without waiting.

They moved quickly through the rooms as the hatches closed behind them.

"Just past the cargo hold, on the other side, is the ready room, then the bridge," he said. It had only three seats, all facing the front. A forward curved screen currently showed a view of the inside of the hangar. The forward screen split as Tom approached it. "These are your quarters. This room can be reconfigured as a small conference room, casual living quarters, or an office."

The last hatch entered the captain's bedroom. A small full bath was on one side of the entrance, and closets and drawers on the other. The smell of bleach was strongest in here. The new mattress and pillows didn't have linens yet.

"Tieg, avatar," Penn ordered.

Tieg appeared as a fit man of 35 to 50 years old with black hair and beard. He wore the same dark blue coveralls that Penn wore.

"Well, I'm off. Lots to do," Tom said and quickly followed with, "He wants what? For crying out loud…" His voice faded into the distance.

"It's bigger than I thought," Penn said.

"It's faster than I thought," Tieg said.

"Uglier on the outside than I thought," Penn said.

"I can remotely control the orbot on board the ship, which will be very useful. Between that and the two small maintenance spiders, this is way farther along than expected. Tom already has maintenance bots scheduled to paint the hull this afternoon."

"I pressured him somehow. I think it's this body. It has a persuasive effect on some men," Penn said. "I don't see how they trusted McDonald so fast. He has a way sketchier past than us."

Tieg continued.

"We're already full on water. The new scrubbers have been installed. Spares were also acquired. Mori provided the standard inventory list for this class of ship. We compared it to the current state, and goods and spare parts will arrive today. Let's get these mattresses out of here."

"Did the standard inventory include guns by any chance?" Penn asked as the orbot grabbed the last two mattresses.

"It just so happens it does," Tieg said. "There's a small armory in the captain's ready room: four Frange Carbines and four 9mm caseless handguns."

"I'll be moving on board today," Penn said. "Now show me this armory compartment."

The approach to Bishop required a total of twelve hours. She followed a series of buoys into the planetary-controlled space, where each one scanned and confirmed their identity. Any other approach would trigger the automated defense systems. They were expected.

After the two required orbits and more scans, Jade was provided coordinates to the Powell estate. During those two orbits, she did her own scanning. It was a Goldilocks planet. It had five oceans, several climates, and no roads at all. The Powell estate was registered as a thousand square kilometers, but it might as well have been a million. No other estates touched its perimeter.

She was given landing instructions that led her directly to the front of the residence. A tarmac to the south of the large residence was concealed from the residence but held six ships of various sizes and configurations. Jade pulled at the collar of her formal captain's uniform as the lift lowered. It was a bit too stiff and tight for her liking.

"Follow my lead," Jeff said.

Six adults and two children waited for them to approach on a perfectly manicured lawn. When they were ten meters from the crowd, Jeff stopped and knelt to one knee.

Let them expel me. I'm not doing that.

"Roman, Sari," Jeff chirped. "I'm back."

The two children nearly bowled the Jeff orbot over. They screamed with delight as they climbed on him while he stood up.

Jade approached and bowed respectfully before the family. "I'm Jade Church, Captain of the *GIN* 109. At your service." Jade had practiced that in the mirror so many times that it was a relief that it was over.

"I'm Powell. This is my wife, Winter. This is Father-Powell and Great-Powell and their spouses Odessa and Rosamond."

Jade bowed again as they did.

Rosamond spoke first. "Your ship. I haven't seen one like that for over a hundred and fifty years."

Jade was amazed by the statement. She'd met some 200-year-olds before but never any so fit or beautiful in their silver years. "I'd happily give you a tour any time you like," Jade offered. Pride in her ship was evident.

"Perhaps after the feast," Rosamond said.

Powell and Winter led the way to the mansion.

Coe watched it all from the *GIN* bridge.

'Feast' was a serious overstatement. It was a gourmet dinner for sure, but the portions were modest and delicious. The dessert was fruit over sherbet with a light sweet syrup. No wine or coffee was offered. The water was slightly flavored with lemon and something else. Jade was delighted with the meal and said so.

Father-Powell and Great-Powell retired to their separate wings. Rosamond wanted her tour, and Winter asked Rosamond to bring Jade around to the veranda that overlooked the lake after her tour.

Rosamond took Jade's hand as they walked to the *GIN*. Jade didn't pull away. "A small word of advice, my dear. If what Powell says is true, you may be back on several occasions with your courier duties. The men of Bishop will be highly attracted to you, but you must resist."

"Excuse me?" Jade laughed. "I'm a troll compared to any of you. I'm short, vulgar but trainable, covered in freckles, and my hair is almost comically red."

"You're an exotic flower," Rosamond said, "A sweet fruit untasted. None of these men have ever seen red hair like yours before. Your figure is equally exotic."

Jade thought about her body in that instant. She had short, small breasts and shoulders broader than most. Her arms were strong for a girl because she had been raised on a farm. Her hair would be a random curly mess if she didn't wrangle it into a French braid.

"Just be wary, child," Rosamond warned.

They were inside the lift before Jade remembered that Coe was in there. When the lift opened onto the empty bridge, Jade pointed out the various systems and screens when she flipped a switch and said, "It even has a ship-wide public address system even though I'm on this ship alone."

She didn't know if it was enough. But she descended to the salon level, and the tour continued as Rosamond told stories of riding in one that had this level configured with rows of passenger seats instead of a comfortable stateroom. Coe was nowhere to be seen.

Finally, they arrived in the reactor room. It was sparkling clean. Polished. Jade couldn't imagine what it took to make it look this new. Coe was not to be seen anywhere.

Rosamond escorted Jade to the veranda where Powell and Winter sat waiting for the sunset. They watched as an eight-legged spider-like all-terrain vehicle sped across the meadow below.

"The children have missed Jeff," Winter said wistfully.

"I understand why. Jeff was part of my childhood as well," Powell said. "He kept my sister and me safe. He expanded our world, just as he will theirs." Powell paused. "And now I know the value of giving my parents a break, just as he will give us again."

"Does your sister know he's back?" Jade asked innocently but knew she'd made a mistake by the instant expression change on Powell's face.

"Rose is no longer with us." Winter was kind to both Powell and Jade with her explanation. Relieving Jade's embarrassment and saving him the pain of telling it.

"Bishop supports lives that are simple and prosperous. Some also find boredom to be a worse plague than poverty. So they gamble," Winter said, watching the sunset. "But what coin can they gamble with that holds any real value in a world where everyone is wealthy by law?"

"Their lives," Powell stated flatly.

"The games vary—all adrenalin-inducing. But the result is the same. The loser dies." Powell spat. "Barbaric."

"How is this allowed?" Jade couldn't help but ask in a world ruled by strict laws.

"Oh, it's not allowed," Winter replied. "Strictly forbidden. All the participants are masked until there is a loser. Only then they are revealed. Their deaths leaked to the net like sick pornography. This shame ups the ante. Increases the risk and thrill. It's sick. Her husband and children had no idea."

"I'm so sorry I triggered a painful memory," Jade apologized.

"No need to apologize," Powell reassured her. "It has loomed large in our minds since we found out Jeff was returning. We will have to tell him. He loved her."

"He doesn't know?" Jade asked.

"It happened right after he disappeared," Winter said. "Two losses back-to-back."

They sat silently as the sun dipped below the mountains, and the sky went from gold to red. In the dwindling light, they watched the children and Jeff return. He ran the lake's shallows, splashing great arcs of water into the twilight. Silence returned as the stars came out. The Milky Way was bright in crystal clear skies.

Powell retired to bed first. Winter showed Jade to her room, where her small overnight bag had already been delivered.

The canopy bed was large and soft, with more pillows than Jade would ever own in her lifetime.

She quickly fell asleep, and it seemed only moments later that she was gently shaken awake.

"Sari, Roman? What are you doing in here?" Jade said to the two children crouching next to her bed.

"You have to save our Jeff," Sari whispered.

"The bad men are here to take him again. The same man as before," Roman added.

"You gotta save our Jeff," Sari repeated, near tears now.

"Don't let them take him. We love him. I'm too small to stop them but smart enough to be sneaky." Roman pulled an orb out from under his pajamas. "If they catch you, I'll say I put Jeff there. You knew nothing. But you gotta go. Momma is having tea in the kitchen. Just say goodbye and go."

"You gotta save our Jeff," Sari repeated.

The two kids sneaked out the balcony door and disappeared in the morning light.

Jade was fully dressed, and the small backpack felt heavy on her spine. Winter was sipping tea in an alcove at the end of the kitchen. It was just 6 am when Jade appeared.

"Would you like a cup of tea before you go, dear?" Winter asked kindly but applied no pressure.

"I should be going. It would be good to get a bit ahead of schedule. Besides, I didn't sleep too well. I finally found a bed too soft for me," Jade said, explaining away any awkwardness she may have been displaying.

"I'll walk you out, dear," Winter said.

As they walked down the steps in front of the house, Jade spotted three hard-looking men in tactical uniforms standing at the corner of the house. In the distance was a Destroyer class ship parked in the pasture—landing gear sunk deep into the soft soil.

"Jade, thank you for all you do." Winter gave her a gentle hug and brushed a kiss onto her cheek.

She took the lift directly to the bridge to see Coe had already prepared the launch sequence. Before she could say a word, they initiated a rapid zenith launch and then, 2 seconds later, a short jump to FTL.

"Whoa there, cowboy," Jade said as they dropped out of FTL two light minutes out and jumped again on another vector for a four-light-minute hop. You just violated all kinds of exit protocols from Bishop."

A final FTL jump for Baytirus, 69 light years away, was initiated.

Coe finally spoke. "I presume Jeff is with you."

"How could you know that?" Jade removed the pack and opened it to reveal the orb nestled in her tank top.

"That Destroyer is designated the *OPAL*. It's registered to Awareness, Inc." Coe was slowing down a bit now. "Father-Powell went out to meet the ship around midnight. And was arguing with a man named Keller. Did you know these skins can listen?

Coe played back a recording. "As soon as you took it last time, it was your responsibility. The cursed thing! Its influence is what killed my daughter. Adventure, adrenaline addiction…" Coe stopped the recording and queued up another.

"They didn't know that the kids were too excited to sleep and had climbed into Jeff's EM, and he was listening to the same conversation," Coe said. "I heard the kids discussing you when they returned to the house just before dawn."

"Shit, we need another socket. They still have the orbot." Jade said.

"Not getting mine." Coe put a hand on his chest.

"The chest socket on my armor." Jade dug the chest, shoulders, collar, piece out of the locker and draped it over the pilot seat. She popped in the orb and closed it up.

"Jeff, can you hear me?" Jade said.

"Thank the makers, Jade. Are you all right?" Jeff asked, "Are the kids all right?"

"Jeff, I'm fine. The kids are fine, but I guess I'll never be going back to Bishop. What the fuck," Jade said.

"Father-Powell tried to use me as currency to buy back his daughter's life. It didn't work."

"Cobb's gonna love this when we get back. My second real courier job and I foul it up," Jade said. "I'm so fired."

"Cobb knows already," Coe said. "The QUEST link is handy that way. Elza, Lita, and Ty are already on the way to Bishop in Elza's stealth fighter. If that Awareness ship is still there when that wrecking crew gets there…"

"Did you tell them about the automated defense systems?" Jade asked.

"I even sent them the high-definition scans I performed on the way in and out."

"Where the hell is Baytirus, and why are we going there?" Jade answered.

"We aren't going there. Don't ever go there. They have a massive automated defense system no one knows about. Almost no one," Coe said. "We'll change course maybe twenty light years out, head for Lumina for sushi. Then back to the Yard. We aren't taking chances."

"This is my ship. I decide where it goes," Jade said coolly. "Course accepted as recommended. And for future reference, I always want an emergency zenith exit plotted, with two random hops programmed every time we stop somewhere. Just in case. And Coe, figure out how to program that sequence into these emergency buttons." Jade opened the hidden compartment.

"Yes, Captain," Coe said without a hint of sarcasm.

"Now I'm going to make French toast," Jade said. "Mind the fort."

"What do you mean they got away?" Penn deflected. "We sent that report minutes after we found out they were going. This was not our fault. There's no way he can blame us."

"Keller does what he wants," Tieg said.

They were in the ready room on the *HELIOS*. Over the last two days, all the supplies had been delivered. The ship had been supplied with sent tools and parts, as well as foodstuffs, mostly basics, frozen and freeze-dried. The outer hull damage had been painted.

"What does Keller actually want? Why do we even work for that asshole?" Teig asked. "I trust you, I don't trust him.

I've seen what he's done to others. He doesn't give a flying fuck about us."

"We've been here for three weeks. We have seen what these people are doing," Penn said. "Are we the bad guys here?"

"Forget what Keller wants," Teig said, "What do we want? We have enough food, water, fuel, and air to last a few years. These naive fools trust us. We can run any time we want."

"But what do we want?" Penn said.

Motion sensors set off some people approaching from the hatch. Teig brought up a cam view on the wall display. They expected Tom McDonald for the final inspection, but Cobb, Elza, Ty Crowley, and Lita Mosley were with him. They were pushing a grav-pallet with a coffin-sized container. On top of it were two heavy metal rail guns.

"Fuck. Are we busted?" Tieg said.

"Relax. Cobb has them on a leash," Penn said. "I hope."

Penn met them at the top of the ramp.

"Well, hello," she smiled as they pushed the container into the cargo bay.

Their faces were all serious. McDonald's looked worried.

"What's this? It's not my birthday." Penn tried to lighten the mood and failed.

"We need to talk," Cobb said and went into the common room and sat at the big table there. Everyone followed and sat without a word. Penn noticed they were all armed except McDonald.

"Please sit." Cobb gestured for Penn to sit across from Cobb, between Ty and Elza.

Penn sat.

"What's in the big case?" she asked, not trying to hide her nervousness.

"Teig? Avatar," Cobb ordered. His avatar appeared at the head of the table but said nothing.

"It's a stasis pod," Cobb said, struggling to start. "Look, something has happened, and we fear it may put the two of you at risk. This is Elza, our Chief of Security, Ty Crowley, and Lita Mosley, also from Security." Cobb nodded to Elza.

"Jade ran into trouble on her courier run to Bishop," Elza said. "While she managed to escape, we realized that Awareness, Inc. may be looking to strike out at us due to recent events. We thought we'd eliminated their last remaining assets. This turns out to not be true."

Cobb continued, "As couriers, you and Jade would be most vulnerable—unarmed ships. Jade is currently taking the long road home. We didn't get there in time before their destroyer left. But Ty and Lita did have a chat with the Powells on Bishop."

"This ship doesn't have offensive or defensive weapons: no med bay, no auto-doc. We brought you some heavy weapons, combat vac-suits, and body armor. They're yours if you want to stay. We will completely understand if you want a different vocation." Cobb looked at Teig. "Both of you."

They were all looking at Penn.

"If you need time to discuss it privately with Teig, we understand," Kira said, her voice gentle and kind.

There was a silent pause for about thirty seconds.

"It kinda sounds like you don't think we can handle it. Tieg, does it sound that way to you?" Penn pointed a finger at Tieg's avatar. "It sounds that way to me."

"It sounds that way to me," Tieg said.

Penn stood. "I spent most of the last hundred years working in an asteroid mining operation. A big one." She began circling the table. "Have any of you ever seen a big mining operation? Because they're only two things." She paused next to Tieg and leaned closed fists on the table. "They're boring and dangerous as FUCK."

"At least this job won't be boring," Tieg added.

"Maybe I picked the wrong body," Penn said, crossing her arms on her chest. "My pick was based on age. I plan to be here a while."

Cobb was smiling wide now. "So you'll stay?"

"Get the fuck off my ship, and don't come back without an auto-doc or an externally mountable laser cannon."

They were all laughing now.

Penn said in a more serious tone as they began to file out. "Cobb, this ship isn't much, but one thing it IS, is fast. Tieg will keep an emergency hop queued up constantly. We won't be filing flight plans and won't take the same route twice. Forewarned is the best defense."

McDonald stayed and helped to secure the stasis pod. It was better than nothing in the event that shit went sideways. The rest of the inspection cleared the *HELIOS* for duty.

Tieg and Penn decided to take her out for a shakedown. An hour after McDonald left, they slid the HELIOS out of the hangar.

They dropped out of FTL in the deep dark and drifted at .31C in a quiet ballistic trajectory.

"Penn, what the hell are we doing?" Tieg asked as his avatar appeared on the bridge.

"I think we're going to bail on Keller. Stay…" Penn replied quietly. "We can't bail all at once. We keep feeding Keller boring reports. Lies even."

"Do you know how many other orbs were working with him?" Tieg asked.

"No."

"Do you realize that the people around that table have killed WAY more people than Keller?" Tieg paused. "A Jovian soldier? For fuck's sake."

"Even if we decide to come over to Cobb's side if they find out about us, we're dead," Tieg said. "And if Keller finds out, that asshole Keller himself will tell them."

"I know. And I have an idea," she said.

"Run? Now? Right fucking now?" Tieg asked.

"No… Jade." Penn said.

Chapter 22: Upgrades

The *GIN* had been gone on this tour for just under a week. By her calculations, the ship was faster than the specs would otherwise indicate.

Jade skipped the return to the Yard for now because the priority was to get Jeff his new body. He'd decided to try life as a human. The *WINTHROP* was gone from the Yard, along with half the wrecks. It was currently parked in the deep dark at some nearly random spot only Coe could find. He described it as touching your finger to your nose with your eyes shut.

Jade slid into the usual hangar on the *WINTHROP*. They were drilling the new name for the *SENTINEL* into everyone. Probably a thousand signs had to be replaced inside the ship. Mori listened full time for the word *SENTINEL* and had a list of dirty jobs lined up for anyone who said it. In just a week, they dropped to nil.

When they got off the lift, an orbot body was waiting for Jeff. Jade dropped him in straight away.

"I have instructions to report to the hospital ring for insertion prep," Jeff said. "Jade, I hope a real hug will be involved the next time I see you. Hunter says hugs alone make all the hassles worth it." Jeff strolled away, and Jade looked at Coe.

"Now what?" Jade asked.

"You have some upgrades scheduled on the new production calendar. I recommend supervising the work. It is your ship."

There was a crew already at the ship when Jade arrived back. There was a long square machine on the deck next to the *GIN*. The supervisor handed her a work order; she knew what this was. She drew the fob from around her neck and activated the cargo opening. An iris neatly opened around the hatch.

The empty compartment opened, and the flurry of work began. A man crawled into the space while the floor panels lifted inside.

By the end of the day, the high-energy laser with optical targeting was installed.

When she thought the day was over, they had her open the other compartment.

They revealed a Custom Hammerhead Personal transport from another crate on that side. It was a two-seater, one seat in front of the other. It fit perfectly. The crew was busy installing the hatch from the engineering-level crawlspace.

"Not every courier stop will have a landing pad," Coe said suddenly at her elbow.

Jade looked up at Coe. "Did I just feel a transition to FTL?"

"That's a good sense of things." Coe was combing his beard with an actual comb he pulled from a jumpsuit pocket. "I'm getting used to the beard," he said.

"Me too. You don't see many beards on professional spacers, and there are many emergency respirators that don't work with a beard."

"I don't breathe. Not really." Coe added, "The blood in my system is oxygenated at the central pump site."

"Where are we off to?" Jade asked. "I know when you hesitate like that, you're asking Cobb or someone what to say. That's fine."

"As long as we're hiding the *WINTHROP*, it might as well be doing something useful," Coe answered. "That derelict station may be Cobb's first special project."

"I'm going up to Ops," Jade said. "Keep an eye on these guys. Make sure they clean up all the crate materials."

Coe nodded and began combing his beard again.

Jade entered the bridge. Cobb was talking to the navigator and didn't notice her. All the stations were occupied, and Mori's avatar occupied the elevated command chair. His avatar was so high-res that he looked solid.

A square-jawed tall man in the uniform of the first mate stepped toward her, saying, "The bridge has restricted access, miss."

"Don't mind Commander Clark, Jade. Ray is new here," Mori said, not eating for once. "Ray was the captain of a fully automated cargo ship. Taking raw ore from various mines to foundries in shipyards is as boring as a plain peanut butter sandwich. He opted for a human body, but his experience is turning out to be invaluable."

"Nice to finally meet you, Jade." The commander bowed formally.

"Nice to meet you too, Ray," Jade said.

"After the uprising debacle, we thought it better to have a second in command with experience and decision-making authority," Mori said.

"This is North." Mori gestured to an orbot sitting at the water reclamation station. "North was a space station orb and would like to return to that role. The plan was for him to take over at the Yard after installing a secondary socket. North would run the Yard. QUEST comms would be a secondary and backup system."

"It's a good plan," North said.

Cobb looked up and saw Jade. He nodded but continued his discussion with the navigator.

"Then *Mr. Special Projects* butted in again." Mori laughed. "He carries a lot of monkey wrenches for such a tiny, underfed man."

"If this twelve-ring station has an orb interface, I may be able to help," North explained as Cobb came up.

"Did they tell you where we're headed?" Cobb asked.

"The dark station," Jade answered.

"We also have three scout ships, including the *TULSA* 471, with orb pilots that are going to survey the colonies you indicated on your map," Cobb said.

"There were four colonies in near space," Jade said.

"Do you Feel like an Other-Duty-As-Assigned field trip with Coe?" Cobb said. "I feel like we have to find a better, safer place to build upon. Elba is very limited but useful. The *WINTHROP* is useful but kind of depressing inside. It's cold and battleship gray. It's a factory and a hospital, mostly. I hope the massive weapons platforms won't be needed," Cobb said. With luck, these could be it. Are you in?"

"Hell yeah," Jade replied. "Gotta field test my new hardware anyway."

The dark station was exactly where Jade's charts said it would be. Cobb went over in the *TULSA* with a cargo bay full of orbots and twelve heavy maintenance suits. The main docking bay in the axle was open the entire three kilometers of the station. Each set of the twelve rings had open hangars. Some had open interior hatches, meaning some areas were in vacuum.

They did a slow pass down the interior of the axle. On the last ring, all the hangars and hatches were sealed.

"We're going to start on this end, drop a few orbots off at each ring, and we'll see what's in that last ring," Cobb conveyed to Ops, where Jade watched with Coe.

POV cam feeds were displayed from all twelve teams.

Cobb was in an HMS when they found a maintenance hatch. He opened the control panel, found a standard power interface, and ran a cable from the suit's chest to the plug. Status light shouted it was already vacuum on the inside of the hatch. The manual release was the old-fashioned idiot-proof kind. Even if he had released the hatch lock, if there had been pressure inside, he wouldn't have been able to open the hatch.

Still gripping the handle on the hull, he pushed, opening it inward.

Jade watched Cobb through the eyes of one of the orbots. He clipped his safety line to the exterior handle, and they began to follow him over. They slid easily along the cable on the carabiners. When all six were transferred and the hatch was once again closed and secured, Cobb opened the valve to equalize the pressure. Once again, this old-school manual method was hazardous if specific procedures weren't followed.

Sounds slowly returned to the airlock. It took a full six minutes before Cobb believed it was ready. He closed the valve and tried the hatch lever. He wouldn't have been strong enough to open it if he'd been in a simple vac-suit. For the power-assisted HMS, it presented no problem.

Atmosphere tests showed the air was not breathable.

They closed and latched the hatch behind them.

Tom had brought up the rear in another HMS. He had remained silent until then.

"This sign says RING 1, HAB 1," Tom said.

"All the other rings are in full vacuum. It looks like an organized shutdown," North said from the bridge. Team Six, Ring 6, has found a map by one of the spoke lifts. Six is a dedicated residential habitat ring. Find a lift, find a map."

"Got it. Heading to Ops in ring one," Cobb said as the HMS easily forced open the lift doors. The shaft was square and looked clear as far as the HMS floodlight could reach. "Reorient yourself now. The spin gravity will get stronger the farther in we get."

All four walls had emergency ladders, and all were put to use. The orbots descended quickly. By the time Cobb had descended the half-kilometer, they had already found the lift on level 1. They entered it from the roof hatch, opened the lift doors, and waited for Cobb and Tom in the corridor. The roof hatch was too small for the HMS, so Cobb used one of the forearm tool pack grinders to cut it big enough.

The main Operations Center was clearly marked on the convenient sign.

"Spread out and see what we're looking at." Cobb pointed at one of the orbots and said, "Dex, you and Tom are with me."

"How does he remember all the orbots' names?" Jade asked out loud.

"Just turn on the Ident layer in your HUD," North replied.

Jade did it with a thought.

That was easy.

She could even see the names and ranks of the humans in the room via the augmented reality interface.

Cobb didn't need to force open the Ops doors. They were wide open. Seven dead bodies sat at the various stations, long dead and nearly mummified in the cold, dry air. Bacteria hadn't survived long enough to rot them very much. All seven had gunshot wounds to the back of their heads.

"We have another one over here," Tom said.

This one was sitting on the floor in the corner. An empty vodka bottle beside him. It was an apparent suicide. A gun was on the floor nearby. There was a sheet of paper in his hand. In dark marker, it said, MAY GOD HAVE MERCY ON OUR SOULS.

"Cobb, any idea what happened there?" Jade asked over comms.

"I think they held out as long as they could." Cobb pointed to the one in the corner. "It was a suicide pact. This one mercy-killed the rest. Then himself."

"They all had bottles. These may have been passed out when the end came," Tom speculated.

"Cobb, we found the rest of the crew, kinda." One of the orbots reported. Instead of trying to explain, he streamed video.

The cargo elevator was piled high with bones. Not bodies. Just bones.

"Cobb." It was another member of the team. He also just streamed video. It was in the massive commercial kitchen. Cobb terminated the feed. The cannibalism was already evident.

Tom plugged in the aux power from his suit into the log server.

"If I had to bet money, it looks like they lost contact with all four colonies." Tom was scanning logs quickly. "They dispatched their last shuttle to investigate. No replies. They waited, but they ran out of food first. Water reclamation lasted longer. They figured out the CO2 scrubbers wouldn't last. Gen 1 scrubbers. They shut down ring after ring to save resources. There were suicides, 'isolated incidents' of starving crews started eating the suicide victims. It snowballed into an organized lottery. The participants put their names in, and the 'winner' was gang murdered and eaten. You were safe if you didn't participate. Suicides ended up 'in the stew pots' as well as the lottery winners."

Tom paused then.

"What?" Cobb said.

"What could be worse than that?" Jade asked.

"When they were all moved to Ring 1, the lottery continued in the largest cargo bay." Tom pulled the power from the computer. "These seven sealed them all in and rapidly evacuated that cargo hold to vacuum. They now had air and food for the next six years."

"OK, everybody, make your way back," Cobb said. "We're outta here."

"Cobb," it was Dex speaking. "I'd like to recommend leaving those of us here who aren't experiencing any emotional horror with the condition of this station. We will work with Hunter to clean this as best we can. Perhaps a few dozen cleaning bots will assist. We clean this up, reassess, and start again."

"I can stay, too," Tom said. "Send a basic shuttle over with a decent fusion generator, and I'll see if I can get the power back on. One of our portables would provide more power than the original reactor in this ring."

"Those cowards!" Keller screamed and threw yet another data pad against the wall in his ready room on the *OPAL.*

"Your emotions will be the end of you." In his office, a sultry, deep woman's voice came from the speakers. "And know that these people are far from cowards. It would be a mistake to presume that. Equipping the Yard with state-of-the-art missile systems is wisdom, not cowardice. Out in the deep dark, the only law there is, is what you bring with you."

"We had it. We had control of the *SENTINEL,* and that wretched Acadia lost it."

"She got greedy," the voice said. "She wanted to return to you in a position of power so she could negotiate an outcome favorable to her. Your treatment of others has trained them to act this way. At least you left the spies to me."

"What's that supposed to mean, Kana?"

"They have no desire to tell me what they think I want to hear. They aren't reluctant to tell me things for fear I'll become angry and lash out. So now we know of the new automated defense platforms under construction in the *SENTINEL* factories. We know of the smart grav-drive missiles that we cannot defend against. We know they're understaffed, under-trained, and spread thin."

"There's a lot we don't know!" Keller was yelling again. "If your spies would do their jobs, we wouldn't be in the dark. Where did they get the QUEST comms? There are less than 300 of them total, for maker's sake."

"We do have some good news. Penngerak has entered the inner circle. She has a ship, and Tieg is the pilot. A courier class Ketch 11. She's done well."

"She?" Keller was taken aback. "I rescued Penngerak from the Nazurn Mines in the Kuiper Belt. That orb was a miner for a hundred years. Are you telling me she took a female human body?"

Kana brought a photo of Penny onto the wall screen. "What better disguise for a spy?" And now she has Cobb's ear. And ALL the Renders."

The word had the desired effect on Keller. Kana was still a fragile orb, but she knew how far she could push Keller.

"Once again, I feel obliged to persuade you away from this course. Vengeance like this seldom ends well and yields little return on investment."

"What good is immortality with a pebble in each of your boots? I could just wait by the river; one day, Cobb's corpse will drift by. But not Lita, or Elza, or Kira, or Ty Crowley. They have ALL betrayed me. They will get their due."

"Only 62 people remain in your once-vast Awareness, Inc. holdings. Care for them, foster their loyalty, and spend them wisely."

"Yard, this is the *HELIOS*, coming in on 283 mark seven as requested. Please don't shoot us. I have the twelve new staffers you requested."

"Acknowledged, *HELIOS*," Ma replied, voice only. "Transmitting a flight path that will take you straight to Hangar 3."

"Will you have time to stay for dinner?" Ma asked as Tieg brought the ship into the hangar.

"Cobb recommended I do," Penn said. "But he also demanded I steal one of your pies or not to bother coming back."

Ma laughed, an honest, heartfelt laugh. It made Penn sad inside.

What the hell am I doing?

Tieg landed the ship in Hangar 3, which was pressurized in seven minutes, and by the time the ramp was down, a young woman had shot over in the zero-G hangar with a guideline rope that ran from the exit hatch to land lightly on the ramp. With a carabiner, she attached the line to a handle by the exit.

"Hi, everyone. My name is Jane, and I understand none of you have any experience with zero-G. I'll start you off slow and walk you through it step-by-step." Jane made a funny. "Maybe DRIFT you through it would be a better way to put it."

Penn watched her distribute belts to everyone, then add a short, meter-long rope to each belt with carabiners at each end.

"Penn will help me demonstrate the next part." She waved Penn forward. "Clip-on. Let the line hang free. Place your hand around the rope, but don't squeeze it. When you launch, it should slide through your hand. Squeeze the rope when you want to slow or stop. I'll go first."

Jane clipped on and launched across. She slowed and stopped when she reached the open hatch and the handles all around it.

Penn took a deep breath and launched.

Way too fast.

With legs flailing, she squeezed the brakes too much and too soon, not making it all the way to the hatch. She went the rest of the way to applause.

"You stay at this end and help them," Jane said. "Clip their lines on here and have them get a seat on that sled."

In the corridor beyond, a personnel transport had about 20 seats.

Jane shot back over and efficiently sent them over one at a time until they were all on the sled and strapped in.

Sled and all, they drove into a freight elevator. It was already in the correct orientation, so when the spin gravity was felt, it pressed them into their seats eventually at 1G.

It was a short walk to the mess hall. The view of the vast yard sliding by as the station wheel turned was spectacular.

Ma and Pa quickly introduced themselves and met everyone briefly. Penn got a real hug. Penn held back tears.

Tonight was buffet style. They got in line. "Did I see a full battery of missile launchers on the way in? I thought Cobb was joking about getting shot."

"Yep, multiple platforms. Railguns, lasers, plasma canons, nukes now, even grav-drive spike nukes. Unstoppable. Long range. No idea where he gets all that stuff. Glad it's here, though."

"The yard is huge," Penn said.

Jane stayed with Penn. "You have got to have the lasagna and garlic bread." There were several other options, but Penn took Jane's advice.

"Where do you get all these fresh vegetables?" Penn asked, watching plates go by. "I've never seen so many."

"We have a farm ring. We grow stuff that's too perishable to transport. Now, with all this help, everything will be easier."

"Farm? In space? Thought you needed land for that, soil," Penn said, savoring her food. "I'm sorry. I've only been a person for a month." Penn paused again. "I'm not supposed to say that. Sorry."

"Look, don't be sorry," Jane said, sipping her water. "Just be who you are. You can around here. I'll try not to be too jealous."

"Jealous?" Penn was genuinely confused.

"You'll get to live your entire life, know the joys of it all. Have kids if you want. A family, if you want, do what you want. And when you're dying of old age, you can transfer to a new body. Watch your great-great-grandchildren grow up." Jane overlooked the impact of her words. "You'll be able to study subjects at a depth I can't conceive. You'll be able to love more because you can love longer…"

Penn got up from the table and fled to the hallway. Uncontrollable tears spilled.

Jane ran after her. "Hey, I'm sorry. I said something wrong. I didn't mean to…"

Penn stopped suddenly. Jane almost ran into her. Penn leaned against the wall and slipped down, gathering her knees to her chest. She buried her face in the cloth napkin from the table.

"It wasn't you, Jane." She wiped her eyes and blew her nose. "The integration docs warned me about this kind of thing. Residual influence, they said. This body may only be 20 years old. But she died, brain-dead anyway. She saved me. Before this, I was a slave for over a hundred years. The cruelty of the cold and endless boredom and toil. I survived all that, perfectly stoic. It's kindness that breaks me. I feel like I don't deserve it. I FEEL like I've stolen all of it. Friends, delicious food, the sheer joy of sleep when I'm tired. Stolen."

"Stolen? How do you figure?"

"This should have been her life. Not mine. I don't deserve it. I feel her. In all the thoughts and feelings I never had before. Residual influence. Her."

"Penn, you honor this girl. Honor her by caring for her. She can't live at all without you," Jane said.

"I'm a horrible person. I've killed people. Worse, I was completely indifferent to people's suffering in the mines. We were all in Hell, and I was comfortable there because I deserved it."

"That settles it," Jane said emphatically. "It's clear I can never be nice to you again, bitch." Jane stood and brushed imaginary dust off her coveralls. She almost hid the grin until she reached her hand out to help Penn up. "Fuck the past. And for the record, bitch, I've probably killed more people than you. Fuck the past. If you made me miss all the pie, I'm kicking your ass."

Jade was not part of the boarding parties assessing the dark station. She watched their progress with Coe in the salon of the *GIN*.

"Are we going to test the new laser cannon?" Coe asked.

"We need something to target," Jade said. "I scanned for asteroids or debris. Nothing."

"Let me call Cobb," Coe said. The call was quick. "Cobb said he has just the thing. He sent coordinates. He said stand by and don't shoot in the direction of the station."

"Be sure of your target and what's behind it," Jade said as they moved to the lift. "My father drilled the rule into me on the farm."

"Good rule, especially if vacuum is involved," Coe said as he settled into the copilot seat.

They didn't have to wait long.

A tumbling shipping container drifted out of the station core axle. In five minutes, it drifted by, and Cobb declared open season.

With a button push, the iris expanded, and the optical targeting system came online. They quickly acquired and locked on the container.

"Firing," Jade said calmly.

Because the container was tumbling, it cut itself in half as it passed before the laser.

"Why can't I see the laser?" Jade asked Coe.

"It's the vacuum. No floating particles to show it."

"It cut that steel like butter. We should haul out a heavy armor ship when we return to the yard. See how it does against that."

"Let's back up and try a distant shot," Coe said. "The optical targeting on this is great. Rock steady. Thanks to the ship."

They shot it several more times until the HEAT warnings came on. "Start a timer to see how fast it cools off to fire again," said Jade.

It was two minutes before they could fire another shot. It caused another two-minute wait.

"The temp is rising in the reactor room. Not good. When we get back, see about some insulation and cooling," Coe said. "I think they're ready to move on to your colonies."

"Maybe I can take the Hammerhead for a spin." Jade was waggling her eyebrows.

Luckily, there was pie left.

Jane had peach pie, and Penn had crumbled top apple. Ma boxed up a blueberry pie to take back for Cobb. When she brought it over, Ma rested her hand on Penn's shoulder. "I'm sorry we didn't get a chance to chat this visit, dear," Ma said. "I'll have my hands full with this lot, and Cobb tells me you'll be back on the regular. I hope Jane has taken care of you and answered your questions." Ma glanced at Jane, "You should have much to discuss. Jane grew up in the Gorham mines."

"You bitch!" Penn said to Jane. "And you didn't say anything?!"

"Eat shit, crybaby," Jane replied, unable to hide her smile.

"You eat with that mouth? You kiss Ma with that mouth?" Penn added, trying not to laugh.

"Ma curses more than any of us," Jane said.

"Leave me the fuck outta this…" Ma said as she walked away.

Penn was back on the *HELIOS* bridge. As they pulled out of the hangar, she asked Tieg, "Are you going to tell me what's in the four crates?"

"Our next job." Tieg was in full avatar, sitting in the seat beside Penn. "Did you know they have QUEST comms here, at the Yard… and Cobb has a portable QUEST Comm unit with him, wherever the hell he is?"

"Wait. No way." Penn ticked off her fingers. "One: those units are so big you need a planet to build them on. Two: they cost more than most planets. Three: there's no such thing as a portable QUEST comm. Four: what's in the damn crates?"

"Look, Cobb and McDonald just called with voice, video, avatars, and data. Conferenced in Pa and some other techs to coordinate loading these four portable reactors and a pile of cables," Tieg said. "Here are the coordinates. Hell and gone from anything. Real-time comms at 20 light years away."

"Well, we'll see what this ship can do," Penn said, shaking her head. "And by the way, the Yard has more railguns, lasers, plasma canons, and missile platforms than any military installation I've ever seen."

"Jesus," Tieg cursed.

"They also have delicious pie." Penn sighed heavily. "Tieg, I don't want to do this anymore."

"What choice do we have?" Tieg said. "If you want to run, now is as good a time as any. Those reactors are worth a lot. If we disappear, these people will think Keller got us. Keller might think Ty Crowley found us out."

"If we lie to Keller and tell him the Yard is vulnerable, he'll walk into a shitstorm with no umbrella."

"What if one of the people we just delivered to the Yard works for him?" Tieg replied. "He'd find out."

"So what?" Penn said. "What can he do? He has one ship left, 62 people, and a handful of loyal orbs. What if they're all just as sick of his shit as we are? What if they all want out like us? You know what he didn't count on? The kindness and trust in these people." She was pacing now. "He thinks trust is stupid. He thinks kindness equals weakness. He's wrong. All those things make these people stronger than him. There's one more thing he's wrong about, and we're going to find out."

"What's that?"

"Forgiveness."

"I'll put together a report on the Yard. In the worst case, he thinks we're idiots and bad spies. Best case, he shows up and gets a grav-spike nuke in the face."

Penn sat thoughtful for a minute.

"Open a private channel to Jane Aldridge," Penn said.

"Go for Jane," came over the bridge speakers.

"Jane, don't say anything, just listen," Penn began. "I can't tell you why, but keep a close eye on the sky. Keep those shiny new missiles warmed up. Nuff said?"

"Affirmative. Jane out." The comm clicked silent.

"The report is on the way," Tieg said.

Chapter 23: Ruins

Jade's ship was the slowest of the four ships that set out to investigate the colonies that appeared only on Jade's map.

The *TULSA* was the first to arrive. It was a decent class M planet with solid jungle and water on about 35% of the surface. It was actively volcanic in several regions, providing plenty of CO2 for the thriving jungles.

It only took two orbits to find the craters from a massive nuclear bombardment. No structures remained. A single remote radio tower ruin was discovered that was now reclaimed by the jungle.

It was much the same story on two of the other worlds. One was cooler and smaller, one larger and hotter, but both of their settlements had been nuked to oblivion.

Jade's survey had different results. A single large city settlement was intact. Large stone structures surrounded a massive freshwater lake that appeared engineered. The city was terraced up on three sides and opened to a valley below on the final side.

Vines had overrun several sections, but not all. Jade picked a spot in the central plaza. Besides Coe, she had six orbots who were eager to explore with her.

"Jade, where did you come up with the term orbot?" Mori asked.

"Hey, don't look at me. I think North started it. They needed a way to differentiate a normal android from one that had an orb driver. An orb robot quickly became orbot," Jade said, checking the atmosphere test readings. "72F and sunny here. Cobb, if you don't want this planet, can I have it? It's a Goldilocks for sure."

"We can share. It's big," Cobb said over comms.

"I expect a city this size could have held twenty thousand people," Coe said. "Maybe more if it extends underground."

"You see that small terrace above the lake? I think it's a warm spring. It feeds into the big lake," Jade said. "Zoom in. There are some kind of small monkeys soaking in there."

"Be careful," Cobb said. "For all we know, those monkeys ate the former residents."

"We'll be careful." Jade had on her Black Badger vac-suit, armor, and a Carbine on a sling. She'd already swapped the frangible rounds for armor piercing.

"Team Orbots, the main objective is to find the Ops Center," Coe said. "Don't linger in any one place staring about. That's Jade's job. Just move through systematically as we create a tactical map of the place. I want all open channels."

The orbots exited the lift and dispersed in all directions. Coe stayed with Jade as she walked across the plaza. It was constructed of flagstone pavers that fit together with laser precision. They approached the wall that contained the lake. The monkeys were one step up in another enclosed pond. Steaming water flowed down rocks at the back.

They were mammals. A few were breastfeeding newborns. The rest were soaking in ones and twos, some grooming each other. All ignored Jade and Coe.

"You know what they remind me of?" Jade asked.

Mori replied in her HUD, "Macaque monkeys."

"Yes! That's it," Jade exclaimed. The monkeys continued to ignore them.

Coe said, "They don't seem to have any predator fear instinct. This bodes well."

They walked along the lakefront. There were stone benches overlooking the water. Leaves had piled deep in some corners, and a substantial tree was attempting to grow into cracks in one of the deeper corners.

They picked a random building to enter, with open doors. Centuries of collected debris nearly filled a café"s outdoor seating area furnished with stone tables and rotted chairs.

Inside, the windows were intact, and birds roosted in the rafters. Bird droppings were deeper than the counter, and the few tables in the room that remained had collapsed.

"Let's try a closed one," Jade suggested. They had to clear debris from the door, and eventually, the rotting wooden door collapsed inward.

It was very dusty, and the collapsing door stirred it up into the still room. It was a garment shop. When touched, the fabric disintegrated like ash before they moved farther in. Jade's comms lit up.

"Mercer here. We found Ops." Mercer had been an orb in an automated Makerbot that built colony infrastructures. Buildings and roads. He had worked alone for sixty years not realizing how bored he was. "There's one body here. A skeleton." The orbot sounded incredulous. "When we walked in, lights came on. There's some kind of power here. Transmitting location."

"My ETA is 17 minutes," Cobb said over comms, unable to hide the excitement in his voice.

Jade and Coe began to walk quickly toward the location Mercer had indicated. It was the top floor of a round turret on what looked like a castle keep that overlooked the entire town. Jade followed Coe up a spiral staircase off a large, dry, open atrium with arched and vaulted ceilings high above. The staircase opened into a room that looked frozen in time.

A large round table sat in the center of this room, surrounded by beautifully carved one-person benches. There were no backs to the seating. The room had a Viking flair.

"Oh, Cobb's gonna love this," Jade said as she looked at the globes in sconces and the recessed lights in an iron-bound wooden ring that hung from the ceiling over the table.

Footprints in the dust and a trail on the table showed Mercer must have walked in here and tested the depth of dust on the table before going up.

Returning to the stairs, Coe turned and asked, "Should we wait for Cobb?"

"Fuck that." Jade pounded up the wide stone steps, two at a time. She shifted from a medieval Viking aesthetic to vintage tech through an open door at a landing.

The room was round and about ten meters across. Windows surrounded the entire tower room just above the built-in consoles that lined the outer walls. Though the windows were dirty on the outside, they still provided a spectacular view of the city. Comfortable chairs were perfectly placed as if they had just been tidied up. The center of the room was dominated by a raised dais where a master station was in the center of its own consoles. The round dais had a counter embedded all the way around that held coffee mugs, napkin holders, straws, stir sticks, and other indicators of a casually run shop.

"Why is it not as dusty in here?" Jade asked.

Mercer replied, "The door was sealed when I arrived."

There was a shelf above the consoles all the way around that made a window sill. It held lighting on the overhang that illuminated the consoles. On two of the sills were pots of soil. Those must have been plants at one time but were completely gone.

"These controls are just like the ones on my ship but aren't in English. I think this one is comms," Jade said, and Coe sent her an augmented text translator for her HUD.

"The language is Finnish," Coe said. All the labels in Jade's HUD were now translated.

"Let's try it." She adjusted the transmission frequency and said, "Cobb, testing the comm gear, do you read?"

"It's weak but working," Cobb replied. "I'm landing now."

"The audio in here is a bit scratchy, but what can you expect?" Coe found another console and began working in silence.

Jade continued around the room. To the right of the door was a bathroom. It had a toilet, sink, and shower with a dozen lockers and a bench. The skeleton was in the bottom of the shower stall. The blond hair was streaked with gray and done in a single long braid. The clothes had faded to gray and were layered but unrecognizable.

Cobb burst into Ops, slightly out of breath. He was looking about with eyes wide. When he met eyes with Jade, he smiled brightly.

"The body is in here," Jade said. "The only one we've seen so far."

Cobb wandered in for a look, but not a long one. He went out and straight up the narrow steps to the master console.

"Find anything yet, Hunter?" Cobb requested as half a dozen orbots filed into the room.

"Yes," Coe replied. "The attack occurred approximately 211 years ago. It appears a chemical/biological weapon was deployed here in retaliation for nuclear attacks. I have the final log entry on video." Coe pressed a sequence, and it appeared on all functioning screens.

A middle-aged woman with bleached blond hair, tan skin, smile lines, and crow's feet appeared to be sitting in the master seat. She was scratching her neck viciously as she recorded this final message. It was in Finnish, but Coe performed a real-time translation through the system.

"It's a bio-weapon of some kind. Clever design. It's probably airborne, and it's probably been here for weeks. It took the sick, weak, and elderly first. Then, the rest of us. Even the remote farms weren't immune." She paused to scratch her collarbone so hard it began to bleed. "It makes you feel like you're on fire, like you're dying of thirst simultaneously. People are just throwing themselves into the lake for relief that never comes. Bodies are now constantly flowing over the dam."

Another bout of horrific scratching ensued as Cobb said. "I hope this bio-weapon is dissipated after 211 years."

"They've always wanted Pratt. Norwich. And now no one will have it... We thought if we sheltered in here with the hatch sealed..." The recording ended.

"This is probably when she fled to the shower." Coe said, "It's a brilliant weapon of mass destruction. The victims dispose of their own bodies. A war between these colonies is obvious. The cause will remain less so for now."

"Coe, this is Waco," came over the comms. "We're the orbot team that was deployed to the East. We discovered an overgrown airship. There's a shuttle parked on the airfield. It's too overgrown to access easily. It's probably the shuttle from the dark station. There are about twenty hangars here as well that we haven't searched. This airstrip appears to be the easternmost point of the settlement."

"Waco, you might as well head back this way. Map some new areas as you go. We will need to regroup and assess," Cobb said.

"Can do. Waco out."

Cobb was silent. Jade was wandering around the room, looking at the views.

"Hunter's title search of colony records doesn't indicate any of these colonies. It's like they never existed. It creates issues and opportunities," Coe said.

"Yes. Yes, it does," Cobb said almost to himself.

"Like what?" Jade asked.

"There's no need, no requirement to be part of the Earth Colonial Treaty," Coe began. "The mutual defense clauses have never been invoked and are considered worthless. Mutual trade regulations are useful to all parties. It has been made so by Earth to bring in trade."

"For now, we will use Elba for official interaction with the coalition. If we move our operations here, I want to keep it simple. We should be able to defend ourselves with the assets we currently have. Keep it simple because we're spread so thin already."

They tried to bring more computers back online for the next few hours.

When the sun set, all power failed.

"Solar collection still functions, but no battery storage remains functional," said Coe.

They didn't notice when Jade returned to her ship for a quick bowl of soup and a night's sleep.

"It's time to kick these fools in the balls," Keller was alone in the ready room. "We can remove one of his biggest assets from the game. His source of ships, fuel, and parts, and now we even know it's one of his food sources. All for just one nuke."

"We haven't received a confirmation report yet," Kana said. We have another asset on site now, so we should wait for his report."

"Tieg and Penngerak have been our best sources so far and our most successful placements." Keller was getting angry again. "I grow impatient."

"You should withdraw and regroup. You need a new base. Somewhere to heal from the last procedure."

"My procedures are my affair," Keller snapped. "I may just remain this way. It limits the pain."

"The sensing of injuries is just damage data," Kana said. "There's also a subconscious component you aren't considering. Memory blockers during the procedures aren't enough. The files clearly say this."

"Enough!" Keller barked. "Stop changing the subject. Begin making your way to the Yard. We will get an update from the other asset faster if we're within the encrypted transmission range."

"Sleep in the auto-doc, at least," Kana said. "I'll begin compiling a list of potential research stations that we can easily take over as a new base and begin to rebuild."

"Do that. I don't care. Not until the last of the Renders are gone."

Tieg entered normal space at .01C as requested. They were in the middle of nothing. The closest star was four light-years away.

Then there it was.

It was an old-style, long axel, twelve-ring space station. The rings were all turning in the same direction. In the dark, it was nearly invisible. Only scans revealed it. Tieg augmented it on the wall display for Penn.

"Tieg, open a private channel to the chief engineer," Penn requested.

"Channel open."

"*HELIOS* to McDonald. Come in," Penn said.

"Great, great, you're here already. Great." Tom was talking fast. Obviously excited. "The axel is open. We're currently in Ring 1, and Hangar 5 is open. A pair of heavy maintenance suits will have their flood lights on to mark the corners. Set down in there. Oh, you have a vac-suit, yes? Yes?"

"I do have a vac-suit. I'll see you in a few minutes," Penn said. "*HELIOS* out."

"I'm turning on all the exterior lights," Tieg said as they entered the rotating axlc. A quick adjustment matched the roll, making it seem like the galaxy at the far end was spinning instead of them.

They traversed the length of the axle on thrusters only. Penn watched the station's interior slide by on the floor-to-ceiling command display on the bridge. Augmented info flowed in, labeling the open bays of the Rings as they passed. A few orbots waved from the open hatches. The two HMS units lit up the hangar bay just before they reached the far end.

They drifted in on grav-foils and set down. Mag clamps in the bottom of the skids secured the ship.

Penn got up, secured her helmet, and tested the seal and comms. "Tieg, let's keep an open channel." This vac-suit was black and had an integrated thigh holster and other pouches for extra magazines. She loaded up at the armory before she entered the small cargo hold and sealed all the hatches.

"Are you nervous? Your heart rate is elevated." Tieg asked.

"Why? Because this is my first time in a vac-suit?" Penn was sarcastic, "Or is it the first time carrying a gun? Or that I totally suck in zero-G?"

"Yeah, that's what I thought." Tieg was amused.

The cargo hold only took 30 seconds to decompress. When she opened the cargo hatch, the ramp was already deployed, and four heavy maintenance suits were already on the ramp.

They began to step forward, but Penn held up a hand, palm forward.

"Hold it right there," Penn said. "You didn't say the magic words."

The Ident augmentation showed that McDonald and three of the five Frost brothers occupied the four HMS rigs.

"Please?" Jay Frost said.

"Close," Penn answered but didn't lower her hand.

"Ummm…" was all McDonald could muster.

"Permission to come aboard, Captain?" came from Michael Frost.

"Granted." Penn lowered her hand and stepped aside.

"Sorry about that… Captain," McDonald replied, watching the first two crates being carried out to awaiting grav-sleds. "I'm just…"

"An excitable boy. I get it." Penn smiled.

"Do you happen to have any food?" Tom asked. "Cobb and everyone went to the planet, and we didn't think. Our suits have plenty of water but nothing to eat. We've been here a day already and don't want to bother Cobb. By the way, this last reactor is for Cobb."

"How many people do you have here?" Penn asked as the orbots were gathering the spools of various cables.

"Just six," Tom replied. "Just the Frost brothers and me. Allan says Hi, by the way."

"I can easily feed you in my mess hall. No problem," Penn said, gesturing a welcome. The sleds were already moving away in different directions.

"No time for that. Cobb wants you on Pratt as soon as possible," he said.

"Pratt?" Penn was confused. "Where's that? Or do I just wander about until I see a sign or something? And yes, we have a whole pallet of protein bars. Will that do?"

"Shit, sorry. Everyone else seems to know everything all the time. I'll send the coordinates to Tieg."

Tom carried the protein bars case out as Penn closed the hatch and repressurized the bay. She left the vac-suit on, as it was comfortable, and the helmet retracted into the collar.

"The database has nothing on the system these coordinates are in." Tieg had the map up on the main screen. "I'm tagging it as Pratt. The system and apparently a planet."

It took them about an hour to get there at their best speed. Landing coordinates came from Coe, Jade's copilot.

"My Ident software even works with comm traffic," Penn said as they slowly descended through the atmosphere at only 300 KPH on grav-foils. "Coe is an orbot. Even though he looks human."

"He's the tall, lanky, awkward one with the long beard and streaks of gray?" Tieg said. "That's kinda creepy. Like Ty Crowley with his skin on. Have you ever seen Crowley not scowling?"

"Once. Lita was climbing him like a tree to get a kiss. She got it. And I saw him smile. He looked totally different. You couldn't pick him out of a lineup," Penn said.

As the clouds parted, they could see the city below. It was sprawling tiers at the head of a valley. A series of lakes and dams were beautiful just below the city. The city was covered in vines like it was the aesthetic choice of the architect. Stone block construction was everywhere and gave the city a medieval feel from this height. The only anachronism was a shining sphere at the top of a round tower that overlooked the city.

The closer they got, the more the ruins became evident. There were many collapsed roofs on the buildings that surrounded the landing field.

An HMS and two orbots awaited their touchdown in waist-high grasses. They were waiting at the bottom of the ramp when the cargo bay hatch opened. None of them said a word. Penn stood at the top of the ramp. This time, in addition to her sidearm strapped to her thigh, she carried a Frange Carbine with a single-point sling across her chest. It rested lightly at the base of her spine.

"Are you just going to stand there, or are you going to say hello?" Penn said.

The HMS didn't advance. Instead, the suit slid open, revealing the driver inside. "My name is Dave Mitchell, and I'm here to pick up the reactor. These handsome gentlemen are Oslo, Ed, and Kirk."

Penn had gotten used to the Ident augment in her HUD and usually didn't pay it much attention. She used it now.

"I thought you were assigned to the *OXCART*?" Penn said as she swung the Carbine around to the front. "Hang on a minute." Her helmet flipped closed, more for privacy than the intimidating look of the mirrored face shield. "Penn to Cobb, come in."

"Go for Cobb."

"Look, Cobb. This is all playing a little fast and loose. Do you want me to just give a multimillion-credit reactor to the first guy who asks for it? Do you have any idea how sketchy all this feels to me? The Ident augment is making it worse."

"What do you mean?" Cobb sounded genuinely concerned.

"Dave Mitchell, it says, is assigned to the *OXCART* for a salvage operation sixty light years away. And one of the orbots has completely wrong name designations. It is just wrong." She was on a roll now. "Would it be so hard to get a short briefing instead of sketchy coordinates to a haunted station with people with no sense of protocol? All that's missing is a scary clown."

"Which orbot has the wrong designation?" Cobb sounded like he was running.

"Oslo is coming up, Remington," Penn said.

"Fuck. Listen carefully. Quietly do an emergency lockdown on the ship. On Tieg. Fuck." Cobb was clearly running now.

Penn remained still. "Tieg is on the open channel. He's locked down."

"Stall, until we get there, but let Dave take the reactor. Oslo was found dead back on the *WINTHROP*. Fuck. We'll be there in two minutes."

"Roger that," Penn said.

"Don't let him take your ship." Cobb said before signing off.

Penn relaxed and flipped her helmet open. "Sorry, Mitchell. I was just checking with Cobb. Sorry." Penn was casually walking down the ramp. "Today has been so fast and loose. I'm used to a metric ton of paperwork, especially on expensive gear like that."

Dave laughed out loud. "Cobb is usually a by-the-book guy, but it's all sideways today."

"Wow, the weather is nice on this planet," Penn said. "Do you know the system name? What's the planet's name? You know, for the charts."

"You should get the regional chart update next time you sync in." Dave was sitting up high on the HMS hood. A movement made him look off to the right. All the orbots looked that way, but Penn was watching the one tagged Remington.

When the orbot tagged Remington saw Cobb racing across the grass, he produced a hidden handgun from a chest pouch. Instead of aiming at Cobb, it raised the gun at Penn.

Penn already had the Carbine aimed. She blew the head off the orbot. She knew it was only the sensor array. She sidestepped as the orbot's gun went off several times, sending rounds where she'd been standing. Her next shot took its shooting hand off at the wrist. Then she destroyed both of its knees.

Dave was finally closed up in the HMS and advanced to stand a foot on one of the ruined thighs.

As Cobb ran up on the scene, Penn still had the Carbine aimed at its orb hatch.

"What the hell is happening?" Penn demanded. Her ears were ringing. She'd had no idea how loud that firearm would be.

"You think I know?" Cobb said. "It looked like it was going to kill you, not me."

Like lightning, someone snatched the Carbine out of Penn's hands, and when she turned, she was staring down the barrel of her own gun at Elza's eyes.

"Does this mean no tacos tonight?" Dave repeated as the HMS opened. "It is Tuesday."

Jade sat with Penn in the common room on the *HELIOS*.

"Cobb told me they would go easy on you to start. Unlike me," Jade said.

"What happened to you?" Penn asked.

"I smuggled in all these orbs, including you. I got kidnapped. I blew up Oklahoma Salvage and almost got killed by the Earth Defense Force. Nothing big."

"I know why he tried to kill me," Penn said. "And I deserved it."

"What do you mean?" Jade said.

"Tieg and I used to work for that asshole, Keller," Penn confessed.

"Keller? You mean that asswipe I crossed paths with on Bishop?" Jade spat.

"Yeah, it was his destroyer, *OPAL*," Penn said.

"I'm glad it's over before we caused anything horrible."

"I still don't get it," Jade said.

"We've been feeding intel to Keller. He wants desperately to kill Lita, Elza, Kira, Ty Crowley, and Cobb. He told us what they had done—horrible things, things that were verifiably true. Not only stealing the orbs. When I got here, I found out for myself. It's true they killed all those people. Tens of thousands on Greco, Vor, Earth, Luna, and other places. Even a squadron of EDF destroyers. Probably more. They betrayed Keller. Destroyed Awareness, Inc. They stole hundreds of billions in credits from Keller on Lumina. Somehow, it all was verified as true."

Elza and Cobb came in from the cargo hold. They left the hatch open, and the remains of the Remington orbot were on the floor in there. Elza set a small case on the table before Cobb as he sat. Lita and Kira joined Elza, standing behind Cobb.

Finally, Ty walked in like a storm. Potential violence radiated from him like heat as he stationed himself by the door.

They all stopped moving at the same time and just stared at Penn.

"What did you do to Tieg?" Penn said defiantly.

Cobb answered casually. "Tieg's fine. There's a failsafe on his orb socket that disconnects it. When Elza was made chief of security, her motto was Trust No One. There were also comm monitors and listening devices throughout the ship, your quarters, and everywhere. Mori hears everything, by the way. All those things are true about us. Minus the context. And more."

"Context?" Jade asked that question.

"We're fighting a war." Cobb said, "I'm told history will call it the AI War. Yes, the *WINTHROP* is a weapons factory. Missiles mostly... for now."

"We won't deny that we can be... brutal," Kira said. "Have been. But we're the ones trying to stop the senseless murder of children. We're the ones fighting against the horrors of slavery."

Lita continued, "We're good at it BECAUSE we can be brutal assholes."

"That brings us to you." Cobb took back the conversation. "Remember, we have been listening. Mori told us you were planning to escape Keller. You even decided you would tell us everything and trust to our mercy. Our... forgiveness." Cobb paused. "Mori has been talking with Tieg while we have been chatting. He has told us everything and opened up for a full, detailed scan. It turns out the only thing he cares about is you. What is it that you care about, Penn?"

Penn looked at Jade before she spoke. "I know I've done awful things. Spying on you is the least of them. What do I want? I want to work for you, earn back your trust, and be guided by people doing the right thing. If I do awful things, I want them to be for the right reason."

"Ty ripped Elza's head off twice. Now that was awful." Jade pointed at Ty.

"Well, Elza did murder me twice," Lita pointed out.

"Cobb got my head blown off at Goris Base," Kira said. "That was not fun and gross."

"Cobb used us as bait and got my ship shot down," Lita said.

"Don't anybody look at me. I'm the saint in this room," Jade added.

"You did blow up Oklahoma Salvage," Elza said.

"Look, Penn." Cobb regained control of the conversation. "I need to be clear. This isn't about regaining trust because we never trusted you. It is about forgiveness."

There was a long pause.

"Can you forgive us?" Cobb asked.

"Do I have to let you rip my head off?" Penn said. Everyone looked at Ty.

"No," Cobb said. "Ty wanted to."

"Ripping my head off was not like smacking a dog's nose with a rolled-up magazine," Elza said, gesturing at Ty.

"There may be more spies," Penn said.

"We know," Cobb said. They've all used the same communications protocols as you to talk to Keller, Remington, and one at the Yard so far. The problem is that we can only ID them if they report in or request guidance. I regret what happened to Oslo. Good catch, by the way."

"So you aren't going to kill us? Tieg and me?"

"No. But Mori will also want to do a full scan on you," Cobb said.

"That will be more complicated because you are in a meat-socket," Mori said over the speakers in the room.

"Don't say meat-socket," Kira said. "It's like the N-word."

"What's the N-word?" Penn asked.

Everyone said all at once, "Never mind."

Chapter 24: Cremation

The planet Hallstead was an independent free market world. The planetary government there had basically two functions: planetary defense and internal security. The highest crime on Hallstead wasn't murder. It was offering or receiving a bribe to a government official. Death penalty for both.

The punishment for capital crimes was life in prison with forced labor—a price so high it was rarely risked. The Internal Security mandate even included threads into commerce. Newcomers often took umbrage to the draconian free market rules. No monopolies for services were allowed. Every citizen had power, water, medical, net access, housing, and food options.

It had created a prospering planet. The competition encouraged makers to create superior products at lower prices. Sub-par services didn't last long. Even the brothels were healthy and affordable for the tourist trade. Credits flowed freely, and everyone remained happy.

The planetary population was approximately ten billion citizens, with an additional four billion visitors for trade and tourism.

Frank Baker was not his real name, but on Hallstead, you said who you were. It never seemed to matter unless you violated one of the few legal tripwires.

Frank Baker was the busiest mortician on Hallstead. Baker End of Life Services were the cheapest on the planet. But only by a little. Several competitors existed, but he specialized in clients who were generous organ donors. Baker would handle all the details for a tiny extra fee, relieving the bereaved families and adding only one day to their cremation schedule.

Emergency Medical Techs on Hallstead would inject medical nanites that would flood the brain of any patient who was listed in the system as an organ donor. These nanites would regulate respiration and heart function until the organs were harvested.

Families and hospitals both appreciated Frank's efforts.

One in ten thousand would be flagged for Frank's special attention.

Special requests were served in these cases. The deceased patient was transferred to a stasis pod instead of the plasma incinerator. An intentional clerical error returned 10cc of indistinguishable ash remains to the family.

Frank didn't care what the medical scientists did with the bodies. The fine print covered his actions.

Fit and young and brain dead were the requirements. He suspected it was an insane cadaver sex thing but didn't want to know, so he never asked. He just cashed the checks and forgot. He never knew that the Morgan Longevity Research Hospital was a wholly-owned subsidiary of Awareness, Inc.

"How soon before we get to Hallstead?" Keller asked Jacobs.

"Four hours, sir," Jacobs replied.

"Sir, I don't think personally visiting Hallstead is a good idea," Jennings said. "Between the strict laws, the constant surveillance, and the total weapons ban, you would be vulnerable."

"We have a hospital there. A legit research hospital," Keller said. He was calm today. "I need the visit. I was headed back to that base to resolve a problem I was having when we found it destroyed."

Keller turned toward Jennings and the entire bridge crew and unzipped his coveralls all the way to his naval. The skin on his chest was gray, with black veins showing under translucent skin. "I'll go in the small shuttle with Lois Ford as the pilot. I need this resolved."

Because the *OPAL* was an armed ship, they weren't allowed to park in direct orbit above Halstead. They were required to park on the far side of one of Halstead's many moons. That moon bristled with plasma cannons, lasers, railguns, and missile silos. Follow the instructions or get vaporized. Everyone followed instructions. The rules were highly restrictive, and Keller had navigated them on many occasions in the past when he was collecting hosts' bodies for his experiments. The loss of the *SENTINEL* and 1800 hand-picked human host specimens was when this all began to go sideways. Chancellor Dalton's incompetence put the program back decades.

Customs was simple if you'd been there before. Ford had only been there on vacation and took a bit longer.

Keller was listed as a board member for the Morgan Longevity Research Hospital. His massive controlling share ensured they did what he wanted, but he'd never asked for anything beyond the supply of bodies for research.

The small shuttle landed on the hospital roof and was met by two doctors and a nurse with a wheelchair. Keller walked past them without saying a word, leaving them to catch up in his wake.

He knew where he was going.

He entered the lift that went down only one floor to the thirteenth floor of the building. That floor appeared on none of the other lifts.

The doors opened onto a vast floor the size of a soccer field. All walls were glass. There were rooms for racks of computers, operating rooms, medical fabricators, and replicators. Keller passed artificial limb labs, empty hospital rooms, and labs of various kinds.

When they rounded a corner, they saw an Asian doctor standing in the center of the aisle, waiting. He had steel gray hair that needed combing and wild eyebrows. His wrinkled face, heavy eyelids, and bags under his eyes made Keller think he was squinting. His long lab coat was brilliant white in the harsh lighting.

"Dr. Zhao. It's good of you to take the time," Keller said as Dr. Zhao turned to lead him away.

"Like I have a choice," Zhao said. The contempt was not concealed. "What's your problem?"

"Improving your bedside manners, I see." Keller unzipped his coveralls.

Zhao recoiled from the smell.

"Clothes, boots, off." Zhao was shaking his head. "On table."

The table was clear, as were all the walls. When Keller situated himself, the auto-doc closed around him and began with multiple passes from a scanner. Many arms descended and washed his entire body. Warm air dried him as Dr. Zhao studied the scans. When the auto-doc retracted, Zhao looked up.

"Mr. Keller. When was the last time you consumed the required nutrients? When did you last rest? It appears you haven't removed those boots in weeks. The soles of your feet were beginning to putrefy. You have several infections that are from small injuries that were neglected."

"Just take care of it," Keller ordered.

"We told you this would happen because of the limited nervous systems. All this numb tissue. Not good. You can't sense small injuries."

"Or big injuries," Keller scoffed.

"Do you want to remain presentable? If so, you need to get… a valet."

"A valet?" Keller scoffed again.

"Want me say nursemaid?" Zhao said as his accent thickened. "Someone to make sure you drink electrolytes, nutrient drinks, bathe you, inspect you for injuries, make you wear fresh clothes. Make you sit. Otherwise, flesh die."

"What about nanites?"

"Medical nanites work based on DNA mapping. Won't work here. Probably make worse." Zhao pulled a couple of drinks from a wall fridge with a transparent door. "Got a valet, or do I assign one?"

"Get the pilot in the shuttle on the roof. Show her what to do," Keller conceded.

"Cobb said you'll be sore for a week," Jade said.

"He just happened to have an orb-doc with him?" Penn replied as they walked back from the *HELIOS* toward Norwich.

"Actually, Ty had it on their new ship, the *TRAX*. He's a Be-Prepared zealot," Jade said. "It's mostly designed to extract an orb from a host with minimal damage, preserving the host. Usually, to place it in their emergency orbot."

"Is that why Lita, Kira, and Elza are always followed around by those scary androids? The ones with dual opposing thumbs and black mirror faces? Intimidating. I want one."

"Play your cards right…" Jade said. The landscape transitioned from a field of grass to a flagstone road. Over the trees, they could see the tower.

"Is that really your ship up there?" Penn asked.

"Yes. It turned out the landing pad up there was specifically designed for that type of craft. Great view, too."

"I haven't seen any of the city yet. We flew over when we arrived," Penn said, "The people that lived here must have been really fit. So many stairs."

"Yeah, the meeting is in the big conference room just below the control room. Up like eight flights."

The conference room was a large, round, windowless room with a thick round table. Over the table was a massive black iron ring that held simple globes for light.

Someone had brought a portable holographic projector and set it up in the middle of the table.

A 3D city model showed the areas that now had power and water. Several people she'd never met were in the room.

"You wanted to see me, sir?" Penn said to Cobb when he noticed her.

"Yes, and don't call me sir," Cobb said as he gestured a man forward. He looked very much like Cobb but taller and slimmer, with a dark crew cut and goatee. He wore the same flight suit as Penn. "This is Jeff Paxton; he hails from Bishop. He and his orbot are joining your crew as copilot. Jeff, this is Penn Marsh. Security has mandated that we all fly in a minimum of teams of two."

"Go easy on Jeff. He's newer at this than you," Cobb said, smiling.

"He does have excellent babysitting skills," Jade joked, but the joke obviously landed flat with Jeff. He smiled and nodded, but the smile didn't go to his eyes.

"We need the *HELIOS* to take a lap. From here, take a load of food to the dark station. We need a better name. It's not so 'dark' now. Drop off the food, pick up McDonald and the Frost brothers. Run them all to the Yard to pick up some more ships that they say will be ready. Jade will meet you there, and all eight of you can convoy back."

"Why the convoy?" Penn asked.

"Safety mostly," Cobb said. "You'll all be escorted by the *HOLLAND*, which will have small ships in its cargo bay that aren't FTL capable and a mobile fabricator."

"The orbot, Remington, that killed Oslo and tried to kill you was under orders from Keller," Elza said. "Your report regarding the state of the Yard's defenses apparently didn't settle well with him."

"I don't understand what he thought the end game was here. It was a suicide mission," Jade said.

"The orbs can still be programmed. Compelled until they can't rise above that programming." Cobb said.

"We didn't destroy Remington," Elza said, "We will study him when there's more time."

"So when do we leave?" Jeff asked, looking at Penn.

"As soon as the food pallets are loaded into the *HELIOS*," Cobb replied. "Probably within the hour."

"Does Jeff know what an asshole I've been?" Penn asked, looking from Cobb to Elza.

"Yes, he does," Cobb replied. "He's under orders to kick you in the crotch if you get out of line."

Jeff blushed.

"I'll give you a lift back to the landing strip. Coe tells me it's raining," Jade said to Jeff and Penn. "Anything else?"

Cobb was in the middle of draining his coffee mug.

"I can't believe none of you drink coffee." Cobb waved as he got up and moved to the coffee urn.

All three climbed the stone spiral steps to the roof. They found themselves under the *GIN*. The rain neatly fell off the ship just outside the tower turrets. They all walked to the low wall that surrounded the roof with turrets. The view of the city below was truly spectacular. There were lights in several buildings below.

"I think we need more people," Jeff said. "Regular people. Families. To make this all work. Otherwise, this city will remain haunted. Empty. Mori told me there are only sixty people assigned here."

"Two hundred seemed like too many when it was just Elba," Jade said. "Then I visited the *WINTHROP*, which can house five thousand, maybe more. Now Norwich. Not to mention the entire planet of Pratt, or the dark station."

"Well, it's not our problem," Penn said. "We just fly."

Inside Penn's HUD, she received a few notifications. One was a manifest of the cargo contents. Another was the delivery orders. Another was the overall itinerary for this "lap," as Cobb referred to it.

Jeff acknowledged the receipt of the files and orders as they entered the lift. Penn was quietly grateful.

Coe was waiting on the bridge, sitting in the copilot seat. An extra orbot stood stoically at attention in the corner. It was different from most of the other orbots because it wore a flight suit that matched Jeff and Penn's.

"Greetings, all," Coe began. "This guy will be going with you as Jeff's bot. The latest version. Hot off the fabricator. I believe yours has also been upgraded, Penn. Wow, are we getting professional or what?"

"Has it got a name?" Jeff asked, noticing the dual opposable thumbs.

"Not unless you assign one." Coe turned toward it, saying. "These have better software. They're smarter and more useful when not occupied by an orb."

A notification popped into Penn's HUD as they began to lift off for the short hop.

"It even has an owner's manual?" Penn laughed. "These are made of carbon fiber? Bullet resistant? Even slightly laser resistant? Should I be nervous?"

"Around here, that may be a good idea," Coe replied.

"You know what the vocation placement people said about this job? 'Boring. With long periods of downtime while traveling.' Let's do that."

"Cobb, why didn't you tell her?" Elza asked him quietly after they were gone.

Cobb sighed. "Too many people know already. The main reason… The new orbot has one of Hunter's orbs so that we can have real-time QUEST comms. That's what's giving us the edge. Elba, the Yard, Goris Base, *WINTHROP* station, Luna, and now the dark station are all linked. There are the ships: The *HOLLAND*, the *OXCART*, the *TULSA*, the *GIN*, and now the *HELIOS*.

Cobb held up the last available steel gray orb.

"But she is already wondering how we maintain real-time comms," Elza said. "She's no fool. The first time it becomes necessary to use it may distract her too much."

"Okay, you're chief of security. What do you recommend?"

"Have Hunter cook up another persona. A bad-ass one. Because if this goes sideways…"

"Do it."

"Ha ha ha…" Mori laughed over the speakers. "Such a decisive skinny little man… Ha ha ha… Done."

Jeff and Penn ran through the rain and up the ramp into the *HELIOS*. They turned and watched the new orbot casually walk. The coveralls it wore shed the water.

When it walked past them into the cargo bay, they were startled by the second one, standing in the shadows. When it stepped forward, it was immediately clear that this one presented as female. Its shape was female, sensual even, and supple in its movement. It was utterly black carbon fiber. The face was black mirrored, but behind the mirror was a pair of almond-shaped eyes, glowing yellow with black pupils that were slitted like a cat, not round like a human.

"Hello, Penn. Hello Jeff," the thing said in a deep, sultry voice. "My name is Dakota." It stepped forward, its hips moving with each step, unlike any bot they had seen. "Besides being Penn's rescue orbot, I'm… crew."

It… she came very close. She was taller than either of them. Her fingers were constantly moving slowly. "I can take care of all the… dirty jobs around here."

The hatch began to close behind them, startling them.

"Penn to Cobb, come in."

Cobb answered before she could say another word.

"No, it was not my idea. It was Elza," Cobb replied. "I presume this is about Dakota."

"We had better security procedures at the mine." Penn disconnected.

Penn moved even closer to Dakota's face plate. "Transmit your emergency shutdown code to me."

The yellow eyes blinked after a moment, and their slits narrowed. Penn received and stored the code in her HUD.

"Now open your helmet," Penn ordered.

The helmet and Penn were nose to nose. It had the face of a woman. She had sharp features, high cheekbones, and short brush-like white hair. Her yellow eyes looked from Penn to Jeff and back.

"Explain or get off my ship. I don't care who assigned you here," Penn ordered.

Dakota's shoulders relaxed, and she took a step back. Her long fingers were still moving at her side, palms out.

Dakota's voice seemed to come from her face, but her mouth barely moved. "You have met Jade's orbot, Coe." Her eyes moved and blinked and her eyebrows moved slightly. "He's also an advanced orbot. His face is organic. Mine is synthetic. He requires a vac-suit to maintain the flesh. I don't. When we return from the lap, Mori said the replacement would have better mouth articulation and look more natural. It will even feel natural. Have you seen Kira's prosthetics? It's based on that tech."

"Why do that at all?" Jeff asked.

"There are places we will go that will be easier to move within if I look… natural."

"If that's the case, get a flight suit fabricated as well. That also explains why you're shaped like that. You look naked, by the way." Penn turned toward the bridge. "Come on, Jeff."

"Penn, one other thing has been upgraded on this ship," Tieg said over the speakers. "We now have a device called a QUEST Relay. And yes, it's exactly what it sounds like. Direct access to the entire QUEST network. It's convenient for a courier. Do you like soccer? Wanna watch live local news from Detroit?"

Penn and Jeff sat in the pilot and copilot seats. The wrap-around screen looked like a window to the outside as the *HELIOS* gently lifted off. The rain had paused, but the clouds hung low and dark.

"Tieg, let's go to dark station."

Chapter 25: Greco

"How are you feeling overall today, sir?" Ford was changing the bandages on Keller's feet.

Keller was staring at the wall display of the stars drifting by. He held up the empty plastic bottle of nutrient drink, and Ford took it, tossing it in the trash with the old bandages.

"I feel… clearer." He looked directly at Ford. "It's your duty to ensure I don't forget. Do you understand, Ford?"

"Yes, sir." Ford collected the trash, turned, and bowed before she backed out of Keller's quarters.

"Clearer," Keller said out loud to himself.

"Kana, how much longer until we reach Greco?" he said to the air.

"One hour and seven minutes," Kana replied cooly.

"Have a tactical team ready in drop ship Alpha. Fully armed and armored." Keller paused. "I'll be going to the planet to do some business. You'll maintain orbit over the city with your launch tubes open and missiles warmed up. If they scan us, I want them to know we mean business."

The dropship landed on the flat just outside the South Bridge Gate. When he stood, all six of his soldiers were prepared to depart.

"I'll be going alone," Keller said. "Your job is to protect the ship. Pilot. Keep the reactors hot for immediate takeoff."

"Sir, this is Greco," the unit Chief said. "Let me take at least a few men to escort you."

"Stay here. Protect the ship." Keller was feeling clear. The clearest since the procedure. "I expect trouble."

"Yes, sir."

"There's a clear vista from here all the way across the bridge. If anyone besides me crosses that bridge and comes this way, you know what to do."

Keller wore a light vac-suit and helmet. It was a bright orange and worn more for the cold than anything else. He knew now he couldn't adequately feel the cold. He also donned a backpack that contained his payload.

The walk across the bridge and into Greco was uneventful. He moved with purpose. His HUD was guiding him to his appointment. The city was warmer with less wind. The streets became more crowded the farther he went into the city.

He was usually the buyer in the past, so he was left alone. Not today. Keller was selling.

Keller entered a ramen noodle restaurant that had seen better days. The lights were dim, and the customers were few. He moved directly to the last booth on the left, where he found the man he sought.

"Hello, Keller. It has been a while," a hard-looking bald man said as he gestured for Keller to sit in the booth across from him.

"I don't have the time or inclination for dinner right now, Haydon." Keller began taking off the backpack. He began to empty it onto the table absently. First out was a pair of hundred round caseless 9mm magazines. Then two handguns with their slides locked back. Finally, a black case the size of a lunchbox. Keller spun the case around to face Haydon and opened it.

Two orbs softly glowed within the case.

"Both are in setup mode," Keller stated. "They can be configured as you see fit."

"Looking for cash or trade?" Hayden said, pushing his bowl aside and drawing the orbs toward him. He looked behind Keller and snapped his fingers. A waitress appeared with an orb diagnostics unit.

"Cash," Keller stated.

Haydon transferred one then the other into the unit and confirmed Keller's claim that these were a rare pair of raw orbs.

"How much?" was all Haydon said, like he was asking the price of a sausage from a street vendor.

"I know these will sell quickly on the open market for at least a billion credits each. But I'm in a hurry today so they can be yours now for 750 million credits cash."

"500 million," Haydon said as he returned the second orb to the case.

"I said I was in a hurry." Keller snapped the lid closed on the case and lifted it to return to his backpack.

"OK, OK. 750 it is." Haydon called the waitress over and said something to her in Japanese.

Keller's HUD translated it as, "Keiko, bring 750 mil from the safe. The biggest credit chips."

Keller stood unmoving until she returned with the credit chips on a small silver tray. There were three. Each was displaying 250,000. Keller scooped them up and placed them in the chest pouch of his vac-suit.

The waitress took the orbs away as she went.

As Keller collected the mags and guns, he loaded each. With one in each hand, he turned and walked away.

"You really didn't have to have all the missile ports open. You're scaring the civilians," Haydon said to Keller's back as he began to walk out.

Keller didn't reply. Once outside, he opened a channel to the Chief. "Be ready. It's about to go sideways. Do not. I repeat, do not leave the ship. No matter what. Repeat that back to me."

"Don't leave the ship, no matter what," the Chief echoed, and it started.

The first shot was a sniper bullet to the side of Keller's head.

Jade hadn't been to Goris Base before. Being on the edge of Sol controlled space made her nervous. The former asteroid mine was dark and abandoned-looking. A single surface structure was visible, but no lights indicated any habitation.

I should have guessed that. Cobb loves places like that.

"*GIN* 109 to Goris Base," Jade said over the comms.

"There's no need for that," Coe said. "We have a node here. Full-time open channel. I'll take her in."

Coe guided the ship around to the opposite side of the asteroid. Jade scanned it as they went. It was an extremely dense iron/nickel mix. It hid any readings of power signatures on the inside.

The *GIN* drifted into the entrance of a massive fissure. After turning a corner, light illuminated the massive interior of the base. A dozen ships were moored inside the base to a lattice of beams, catwalks, lights, and gangways. Large automated spider-like bots were disassembling some ships while most other ships were in various stages of restoration.

The *GIN* moved toward the main dock, where dozens of shipping containers were neatly stacked. A standard docking collar extended, and the *GIN* settled down onto it.

"How many people are stationed here?" Jade asked.

"Current compliment is thirty-one. Mostly junior crew, engineers, mechanics, and logistics. The base commander is currently Ruth Phillips. My brother on duty is Dennis."

"Brother on duty?" Jade smiled, looking at Coe.

"Another Hunter persona," Coe replied.

"Do you know why they're mothballing this base? Reducing it to a skeleton crew?" Jade asked.

"I wouldn't call it mothballing. Not even a skeleton crew. Goris base functioned for years with fewer people. The six that plan to remain will keep the base going as a supply depot, a waypoint, and salvage operation."

"Four of these ships will fly with us to Elba. They're all fighters with FTL capability. They will be added to the Elba Security Team. We have loaded them up with materials that will make Nathan Wells, the governor of Elba, happy. For now."

"Who are the people we're taking? What's the cargo we're moving?" Jade asked. She should have asked all this earlier.

"We will be taking tools and instruments for the engineering team at Elba," Coe said as he got up.

Taking the lift down, it opened directly into the gantry. They proceeded to the airlock as it was opening from the other side.

Ruth greeted them with a bow and led them into the base. Every corridor was concrete, broad enough to drive a car and obviously made by those massive automated maker machines.

Keller's head was rocked to the side by the bullet. He stumbled for a step and turned in the direction of the shooter. The fool was so sure of himself that he had sat up behind his concealment.

Keller still had a gun in each hand, and the targeting system in his HUD fired the instant his gun reached the center of the shooter's face.

He kept walking as if nothing happened.

Every ten paces or so, another person would fire on him and then die an instant later.

The farther he went, the more rounds hit his center mass to no effect. His outer flesh was paying a horrific toll.

Keller opened a channel to the drop ship. "Do NOT leave the ship. Protect it at any cost. Be ready to take off."

Keller took a round far too near the credit chips in his pocket when he realized everyone in the street was trying to kill him. So he began to kill them all preemptively. His aim and range were far better than theirs. By the time he reached the bridge, the firing had nearly stopped.

The dropship was in the air before he reached the top of the ramp.

"*OPAL*, Red Alert. I expect trouble. I'm sending the coordinates now. I want a precision Javelin there the moment we're onboard."

"Acknowledged, sir." A moment later, "Javelin is standing by."

The jump ship pilot was very good. He came in hot and set down secure without concern for a few bumps to his soldiers on board.

An instant later, "Javelin away."

If Haydon were smart, he would have moved out as soon as I left him.

Keller knew the ramen shop would be rubble by the time he reached the bridge. Maybe the building to each side as well, but that was Haydon's fault.

The crew did a commendable job hiding their reactions to his condition.

"Mr. Jacobs, best speed to Mars."

"You need to focus, little man," Mori said from a lounge along a wall of the conference room. He was dipping long breadsticks into a large jar of peanut butter. "I'm having more coffee sent in."

"Where are we on hardening the defenses?" Cobb was studying 3D representations of the dark station and the planet Pratt.

"The fabrication factories are working at full capacity. All 64 satellites for Pratt will be done in four days," Mori said. "Why are you rushing to move everyone here?"

"We have resources here. We have enough people. With the new staff at the Yard and on the *OXCART*, we're restoring more and more salvaged ships." Cobb turned to look at Mori.

"What is it you want? Really?" Mori asked. "We can get it for you. We have enough credits to pay everyone's salaries forever."

"I want peace, time, the ability to research and create new tech, good food, and good coffee. I want Kira to be safe, and I want everyone to be safe."

Chapter 26: War

The hatch slid open, and Ty was followed in by Lita. Cobb looked up from the holographic display. Both Lita and Ty had a strange look on their faces, a look he'd never seen before.

"What's up?" Cobb simply asked.

"Are we at war or not?" Lita asked as she leaned on the holographic table. "What the hell are you doing? Are you playing house? Do you have new toys to play with, like Dark Station? What?"

"Mori was just asking the same question." Cobb turned off the display over the conference table. "It seems like five minutes ago, I was just a salvage engineer making money to buy parts to upgrade the *TULSA* 471. I love that ship. It represented freedom for me. I was just a guy who finally had everything I'd ever wanted. Good food, great coffee, and enough money to never worry again. I fell in love, and shit really got weird." Cobb stood and slowly began to walk around the large round conference table. "The woman I love got her head blown off. And didn't die." Cobb was moving slower but still moving. "Kira never told you that story? Never described the look on my face when I saw just the lower jaw hanging from what remained of her neck?"

Lita took a step back.

"The *SENTINEL* was just salvageable after that." Cobb stopped when she backed into Ty, who stood there stoically. "I found out the truth after that from Kira and Cruze. About Awareness, Inc., the Render program, its horror, and the events on VOR that ended all the AI orb production."

"Come no closer," Ty warned, holding a hand up, palm out. Cobb ignored it. He still moved closer like a clock's minute hand.

"I thought it was over then," Cobb said. "I had Elba legally. I had the *SENTINEL*. I even owned Oklahoma Salvage, the Yard, and Goris Base. It was more than enough. But the universe was not done with me. Cruze, Kira, and fucking Constable Locke drew me back in. My part was easy, they said. They trusted me because I didn't need the money, plus I had the *SENTINEL*. A hospital specifically designed to let the orbs be human again."

"It's only 260 orbs," Lita said.

"NO!" Cobb raised his voice for the first time. "It's 260 PEOPLE. And like people, some of them are assholes. Big enough asshole to want to kill people I love. So I became more like YOU. I went from the joy of working on my ship and finding nice rugs for its lounge to nuking people because I was pissed off. Using my *SENTINEL* factory to make weapons satellites instead of weather and comm satellites. To restore fighters and not automated farming bots."

Cobb pounded the table and the planet Pratt came up alongside the *WINTHROP* and dark station.

"Yes. I know I'm still at war." Cobb was quiet again. "I'm circling the wagons. Do you know what that means? I'll harden the defenses around these hidden assets so that I can stop worrying about them. Then I'll go hunting."

"Your plan has a flaw," Ty spoke in a low rumble. "People you care about are at risk. The weakest of them you care for the most. That gives your enemies leverage."

"What do you recommend I do?" Cobb asked.

"Keep them close. Protect them fiercely… and release the hounds."

The conference room door slid open just then. Elza walked in with two of the black advanced orbots.

"Did you tell him yet?" Elza asked as one of the bots stepped up to Lita's elbow and froze like a horrible statue.

"Tell me what?" Cobb looked at all three.

"We are the hounds," Ty said.

"Time to get the band back together," Cobb said.

"We have a change of plans," Coe interrupted Ruth, giving a tour of the refurbished Command Center on Goris base.

"Oh?" Ruth said.

"Full evacuation. Mothball the base. Even Dennis will go," Coe said. "We will take every ship that can fly."

"The ore freighter and the yacht *WEBSTER* can only be flown by AI orbs, and The *WEBSTER* isn't airtight," Ruth said.

"Full evac," Coe said. "I'll fly the *WEBSTER*."

"And I'll fly the ore freighter," Dennis said.

"We need this place dark in two hours," Coe said. "I have the coordinates. We will all rendezvous here, and then the final coordinates will be given to everyone. We need to keep those coordinates off all the Goris Base computers."

Rapidly, everyone was assigned a ship and a crew. The *HOLLAND* showed up, and four shuttles were loaded on board. Ruth was not a pilot, so she was assigned to ride with Jade. Jade was the first one ready to launch. There would be sixteen ships in their convoy, and they all had to exit the base one at a time. The *HOLLAND* stood on red alert to protect them as they exited.

Coe was the second to arrive in the luxury yacht at the rendezvous point. The yacht looked like it had a bite taken out of it where the glass windows surrounding the bridge had been blown out of the ship.

"Dennis will be the last one out, and we need not wait for him. That hauler will be super slow. It will hit FTL, but only barely."

Four of the ships were FTL fighters that went directly to Elba as previously planned, but the rest headed for Pratt.

"Can you tell us what has happened, Coe?" Jade asked over comms.

"It looks like we're retreating to safety until the grown-ups handle a problem," Coe said over the comms. "They're also evacuating all nonessential personnel from Elba. Ty and Lita are going to Elba in *TRAX*. Which now has two belly-mounted missile trays."

"Wells is going to love that," Jade said.

"Where's Cobb?" Jade asked.

"He and Kira left in the *TULSA*, and Elza left in her ship," Coe said. "Did you know she renamed it *REAPER*?"

"No, that's not subtle at all," Ruth said.

"Did they say where they were going?" Jade asked.

"Hunting was all they said," Coe answered. "Ivy will keep an eye on them."

"Kana, I want to land in Holden on Mars," Keller said from his seat in his ready room. "At the spaceport. It's a legit visit. Take on food, water, and new scrubbers. Is there anything else we need? We have the credits."

He was fresh from the auto-doc. It had done what it could. He sat naked in the chair, looking at his left arm. An explosive round to the bicep tissue on that side had caused severe damage to flesh, and all the flesh below that had to be removed until the feeding system could be repaired. It was the bare combat chassis.

"Should I pay the crew?" Kana said. "I don't recommend shore leave. Too close to home. We can't afford runners."

"Remind the logistics people that their wristband is a monitor AND an automated kill switch."

"I'm on the grid now. I've been looking for all traces of Cobbal Blocke in the system," Kana said. "The shipyard on Earth is vacant. Patrol bots have been hired. The Oklahoma Salvage offices on Freedom Station are still open but inactive. There's a remote base on the Luna as well."

"Are those places active?" Keller asked. "Do we have any contacts on Freedom Station?"

"Yes, the Satsujin syndicate. But it will cost," Kana replied. He also has a registered salvage claim on an asteroid mine called Dressler, renamed Goris. There have been lots of encrypted communications between those locations."

"Do we have any more long-range stealth smart missiles?" Keller smiled and looked at his polished hand.

"Yes, sir," Kana replied. "We do."

"Here is the plan," Keller began.

"What do you mean? Gone?" Cobb said to Harv Reardon over comms from Luna.

"It was a simultaneous stealth missile strike to the Hangar base on Luna and the OS Yard in Oklahoma—low-yield nukes. Plus, there was a bombing in the offices in Freedom Station. No casualties, but 37 were injured on the station."

"Are you sure no one was killed?" Cobb could only look at Kira as he spoke to Harv.

"I was lucky not to be at either of those places. Ian left a few days ago, heading your way with his fancy fabricator," Harv replied. "What do I tell them when they find me? These aren't idiots. Boy, Ian is going to be pissed about his new ship."

"Tell them the truth," Cobb said. "But don't let them arrest you. If it gets sketchy, get to Lumina. The *OXCART* is headed back from the outer reaches and can meet you there."

"I don't think I'm going to hang about and wait," Harv said. "Jesus, Cobb. I just wanted to retire in peace."

"We'll get you there," Cobb said.

"Be safe, old man," Kira added before they disconnected.

"Love you too," Harv said. "And Cobb, fuck you."

"Cobb to Lita, come in," Cobb said over comms.

"I gotta give you credit, Cobb," Lita said over the comms to shouting in the background. "Nathan Wells has got real balls. He's actually yelling in Ty's face. And Ty is letting him. Wells was not hearing the part about essential personnel."

"Elba has already told the population they were evacuating as soon as the *HOLLAND* gets here," Cobb said. "They're already evacuating Goris Base. That and Elba are the last of the places with my name on them."

"Can you contact Elza?" Lita said, looking at Ty as Wells fell silent. "Might be nice if he came to us for once."

"I'm trying. She has everyone else moved to your retreat. We'll all be back at the *TULSA* soon after. Have the bay open. We'll back the REAPER in."

Jade landed the *GIN* 109 on the tower pad. As expected, Ruth was suitably impressed with the city.

"You said you found this?" Ruth asked as she wandered around the control center, which buzzed with activity. Techs were replacing some consoles and repairing others. The elevated master console looked like it was completely replaced. It was now surrounded by modern halo-display and HUD windows.

All the surfaces had been cleaned, even the windows.

"What do you plan to do with your new world?" Ruth asked, her expression serious. "Your defense platforms are nearly ready. By the way, where did you get so much U235? The EDF has a tight lock on its distribution and use."

"The SENTEN… I mean, the *WINTHROP* collected tons of it from the fleet wreckage. It's been cranking out missiles ever since. Have you seen the size of its automated factory?"

"Nice of Cobb to set up your defense grid. You got a contract for that? For all these upgrades? I always liked to have everything clear, you know. In writing," Ruth said. "Just because it's happening fast doesn't mean it's unimportant. What exactly do you have in writing?"

"Well, I'm a courier," Jade said.

"Well, I'm the materials salvage specialist," Ruth said, looking out the window. Neither of us is doing our jobs right now because they're protecting us. We are liabilities. We can be used as leverage if these fuckers ever get their hands on us."

Ruth looked at Jade then. "These people that are protecting us are killers, savages, assassins, soldiers, and if we're lucky, they're worse than our enemies."

Jade didn't know what to say.

A generic orbot entered the control room and approached Jade.

"Hey, there. Get me back in my body before I forget how to walk again," Coe said in a voice with a blank face.

They left Ruth looking out the windows and returned to the salon on the *GIN*, where Coe's body sat in a chair with its eyes closed. He was sleeping, for all the world knew.

The orbot opened its chest and presented the gray stone-like orb. Jade lifted it and studied it a moment. She then unzipped Coe's coveralls and touched the access control. The socket opened and she dropped the orb into it.

Coe opened his eyes like he'd just woken up. Before he could do anything, Jade spoke.

"Are you here to protect me?" Jade was standing over him. Coe stalled for time, zipping up his coveralls.

"Among other things," Coe said as he slowly stood. "Like comms. Comms are super important."

"Why doesn't Penn have a bodyguard?" Jade asked. "She's a courier, too."

"Jade," Coe said. "She does have a bodyguard. Her name is Dakota. She's not off to a good start..."

Coe's face froze.

Chapter 27: Vengeance

"Sir, you have to drink this," Lois Ford said to Keller. "And you have to return to the auto-doc. I'll come get you before we arrive."

Keller watched her cower even as she said the words. He drank the liquid, thinking of how weak the flesh was. He wondered for the hundredth time if he needed it at all.

"Sir, where are we going?" Ford asked. "The crew would function better if they knew the plan."

Keller looked at her then, and she went silent. He wondered who was feeding her these questions for him. He stood and zipped his flight suit closed. Ford was frozen where she stood, and Keller pushed her aside.

"When we reach the coordinates, I want three heavy missiles ready for launch. We will be doing little more than a fly-by. It will send Cobb and his crew another message."

Keller exited the bridge to spend some more time in the auto-doc and think, planning several moves ahead.

Penn and Jeff sat in the pilot and copilot seats as the *HELIOS* approached the dark station.

"It's going to need a new name," Penn said. "It's not so dark now."

Ring One and Two had power and were bright, with lights from all the windows. As they entered the central axle, it was completely illuminated.

"How the hell can all these lights still function? Didn't this thing sit vacant for like 200 years?" Penn asked.

"They were made to last," Dakota said. "Back then, there was no resupply."

"*HELIOS*, Hangar twelve, please," came over the comms.

"Roger that," Tieg replied, "Please inform Chief Engineer McDonald that we will depart as soon as we're unloaded."

A dozen orbots were waiting for the *HELIOS*, and the unloading was done in short order, made easier by the weightlessness in the axel.

They had to wait for McDonald to don his vac-suit and come over from Ring One.

Once he was onboard and the ship pressurized, he entered the bridge. The ship had already left dark station and was transitioning to FTL.

Penn and Jeff stood to meet McDonald but backed away as he removed his helmet. The smell was terrible.

"Tom, it's nice to meet you but get the fuck off my bridge," Penn said, folding her elbow across her face.

"What happened?" Jeff was a bit more polite.

"I've spent the last nine days in this vac-suit. No showers, no suit cleaners, no working toilets, no fresh clothes."

"I'll take him," Dakota said. "I'll get him in the shower, toss his clothes in the recycler, gen up a new jumpsuit. And put this on in the cleaner and run it twice."

McDonald followed her out, apologizing all the way.

Dakota suddenly stopped, and McDonald ran into her back. It was like hitting a bronze statue. She slowly turned back to the bridge hatch, sweeping McDonald to the side as she did.

"There has been another attack." Her voice was urgent.

"Coe, are you all right?" Jade asked, having never seen him glitch like this before.

When he began to move again, his eyes turned to Jade.

Saying nothing, he drew out his comb and combed his beard. He was stalling, Jade knew.

"What is it?" Jade demanded.

After a moment's hesitation, he said. "There has been another attack."

"I think Cobb expected it. I'm glad we got everyone out of Goris Base in time," Jade said.

"It wasn't Goris Base," Coe said. He gently held Jade's shoulders. "It was Kibler… your parents' farm."

Jade's eyes went wide. An instant later, she wrenched free and was in the lift and up to the bridge.

By the time Coe exited the lift, they were away. The emergency zenith launched and transitioned to FTL as soon as they reached the vacuum of space.

"How long ago?" Jade demanded.

"65 seconds," Coe said. "Kibler had a hunter orb in your parents' command center, designing the next dome with the people Cobb sent to help your parents. A ship dropped out of FTL over the planet. They had just hailed them when they detected missile launches. It was over before he could broadcast a warning."

Jade was focusing on the controls now as Coe sat in the copilot seat.

"Jade, we've never tested the *GIN* with all twelve reactors on full. Your inertial dampeners don't have the capacity to counter an unstable grav-field at this speed," Coe said in a calm, reasonable voice.

"Get Cobb on the fucking comms. NOW!"

Coe activated the comm channel instantly.

"Jade, Kira, and I are closer than you in the *TULSA*," Cobb said. "We will meet you there."

"Cobb, was this Keller?" Jade said, barely able to breathe.

"Yes."

"Did he find them because of you or me?" Jade whispered.

"All this is my fault," Cobb said.

Jade disconnected the comms.

"Keller must have gotten my name from the Powells on Bishop," Jade said quietly. "I saw Cobb covering his tracks. Why didn't I cover my own?"

"There's nothing I can say," Coe said, but his tone conveyed sympathy. Jade felt it.

"I need sleep. I'm emotionally exhausted. I am not going to think. Call me when we get there." Jade left the bridge as Coe backed down the power 10%.

The *HELIOS* returned to Norwich on Pratt.

McDonald was showered and in a fresh set of clothes by the time they arrived. He still needed a shave. He studied the display as Cobb flew over the site on Kibler.

"It looks like three detonations in the low atmosphere were designed to cause maximum destruction."

Coe was providing a wire diagram overlay of the original compound. It was just a few domes and buildings, now replaced by craters.

"Why would Keller pound the rubble like that?" Penn asked. "One would have been enough. He's killing a fly with a sledgehammer. Using three blows."

"It's a message for Cobb," Dakota said. "He's hurting the people Cobb cares about."

"Coe, what's the status of the defense grids on Elba, the Yard, and Pratt?"

"The Yard was already armed up. Adding all those long-range missile batteries ensures no one is sneaking up on them," Coe said. "Elba is such a small installation on such a small island. Automated defenses were easy there. Wells and the six remaining staff have all moved to the retreat residence there, just in case. The sixty-four sats in the defense platform over Pratt are all active. The *WINTHROP* is stationed just off the shoulder of the dark station. Add to that no one has the precise coordinates for that station but Hunter. Even if Keller knew it existed, he'd never find it."

"Keller has one ship," Penn said. "I also think he's insane from experimenting on himself."

"What kind of experiments?" McDonald asked.

"I don't know," Penn said. "It's the real reason he was collecting orbs. Not for the money."

The airfield was covered with ships when they finally returned. No two were the same.

"Why is the *HELIOS* painted white? I kinda like that camouflage pattern on that ship near the edge," Penn said.

"In civilized regions, where there's a lot of traffic, being highly visible is good," Coe said. "Have you ever flown in space around Earth? Air traffic control there is a nightmare."

Jade set down the *GIN* just outside the cave where she originally salvaged it. She'd emerged from her nap, armed and in her armored vac-suit. The *TULSA* 471 was already parked there. It was on a plateau just at the edge of the devastation.

Jade's flyover before landing might as well have been on another planet. Nothing remained of the farm she grew up on. She'd remained stoic until the airlock door opened into the *TULSA*, and Kira was there, her arms open.

Kira ignored the body armor and the rifle slung at her back.

Jade sobbed as Kira held her. Kira didn't have to say a word. She just held Jade.

Cobb quietly conferred with Coe. When they were done, Coe put his helmet back on and left the *TULSA*.

"Is it all right if Coe flies the *GIN* back to Elba? You can fly with us," Cobb said.

"I think it's a good idea," Kira added.

Jade couldn't speak. She just nodded.

With a thought, the *TULSA* lifted off as Cobb entered the bridge. Ivy, the *TULSA's* Hunter persona avatar, was there in the command seat. Elza and Lita occupied the navigation and communications stations. Ty stood to the side like an angry statue.

"It will be Goris Base next," Cobb said. "I thought he'd go there, not Kipler."

Kira entered the bridge, Shaking her head. "She's shut down. I put her in our quarters." She looked at the tactical display. "Goris Base, you think?" she said.

"Has to be. I also think he knows we know," Cobb said. "What he doesn't know is that it is empty."

"His hubris will want a conversation first," Elza added.

"Well, it's our job to deny him what he wants," Lita said.

Cobb's ship was faster than any of them could believe. They were less than an hour out when the sensors on Goris Base detected a ship coming in.

It was the *OPAL*.

It slid inside the base like it had been there a hundred times before.

"I know you're out there, Cobb," Keller said over comms. "I also know Elza is with you because she never goes anywhere without her REAPER. Kira is probably there because you can't do anything without her. That leaves Lita and Crowley. I'd bet money you brought those attack dogs as well."

Cobb dropped out of FTL at a distance.

"ETA 25 seconds," Dennis said over comms.

Cobb made no reply. Ivy mapped the advance of the Ore freighter on tactical. It was moving on a precise course at 1.25C being flown by a lone dark gray orb. It was fitting that Dennis Goris was the persona. The base was named for him, after all. The impact vaporized Goris Base, the *OPAL*, the entire asteroid, and a massive region around it.

"Sensors will pick that up all the way back to Earth," Dennis said as his avatar appeared on the bridge.

"Who gives a shit," Cobb said. "Honestly, I don't think I'm ever coming back to Sol. Let's make for Elba before Wells has a nervous breakdown."

"Jade, wake up. This is Coe. I'm on the *GIN,* almost back on Pratt." The comms chimed, "You have entered orbit around Elba, and Cobb has detected some kind of satellite in a geosynchronous orbit."

"Why are you telling me this, Coe? They will handle it. They always do." Jade sat up.

"It's my job to protect you. Do you have a vac-suit on?"

"I'll be fine; they will protect me," Jade said, noticing the Grendel just sitting in a chair, unsecured. "Look, Coe. I need to put the Grendel back in a locker. It's dangerous even to hold it on a ship. What's happening?"

"Scans indicate that this three-meter square cube is being held in orbit by simple grav-plates. No radiation, no explosive detected, no life signs."

Jade heard, felt, a loud sound, a thump.

"What are they doing?" Coe asked as if it was a literal question as she picked up the rifle and started to the cargo bay and the small locker room.

"Ty is suited up and is about to go and check it out," Coe narrated over comms. Jade knew Coe was just trying to occupy her thoughts. Distract her. "The *TULSA* is stationed a thousand meters back. One of the hatches is open on the cube. A pedestal console is inside. Ty's going in."

Jade entered the cargo bay and noticed an unusual light in front of the REAPER. She walked right up and looked down a hole in the cargo ramp into another ship.

We've been boarded!

"Coe, tell Cobb…"

Jade was taken off her feet by a blow to her face and head. She crashed hard into the bulkhead. She never heard or felt her left arm break with the force of the impact. She collapsed, unmoving to the floor, with blood pouring from her nose and mouth.

On the bridge, they watched Ty reach the sat. He examined it on all sides before entering the open hatch. The raised console in the center came to life.

"It looks like a comm relay. We would have never detected it if that hatch hadn't been left open."

They could see Ty through the open hatch using the long-range optical. They saw Ty look up and say, "Cobb, there's a…" The hatch slammed closed, and the entire thing began to accelerate at high speed away toward the surface.

Then it exploded.

"Elza, can the REAPER catch Ty before re-entry?"

"We will find out!" Lita said as she followed Elza out. "He'll be so pissed if he lands in the ocean. Again."

"Cobb, there's something wrong," Coe said on a broadcast channel for everyone.

Then the lights went out.

Chemical emergency lights glowed to life.

Elza and Lita entered the cargo bay and froze.

Not because they saw Jade's body on the floor. But because they couldn't move.

Keller advanced from the shadows, holding a weapon that was hot and recharging.

"I've been waiting too long for this. It required many orbs and many bodies before I got it right. EMP alone didn't work. But I have you now." He walked up to face them. "I was going to take you and make it last, but I don't trust any of you." Keller swung a sword at lightning speed, and Elza's head flew off, followed by Lita's. Their bodies collapsed to the floor in great gushes of blood.

The bridge went dark. Ivy disappeared. Cobb had no senses outside his own body for the first time in years.

"It was a heavy EMP set off inside the ship. Get Jade. There are six escape pods. All their hatches open automatically if power is lost." Cobb opened a panel and handed a Carbine to Kira. Both had armor-piercing rounds. "Get Jade, and I'll be right behind you. I'll go after Lita and Elza."

They split into different directions. Kira ran, and Cobb stalked his way toward the cargo bay. Cobb was not fast enough.

Rapid fire could be heard ahead. An entire mag dump. Then quiet. And then worse... laughter.

Nooo... I recognize that voice!

When Cobb rounded the corner, he saw Keller standing in the center of the cargo bay, surrounded by bodies. In his hand, he held Kira's head by the hair.

Kira...

Cobb opened fire.

He alternated between headshots and body shots when nothing worked. He focused on his knees. Keller went down just as Cobb's ammo ran dry.

"You're such a fool, Cobb." Keller laughed. "So predictable. Why do you think I was experimenting with orbs? To find a way to detect and destroy them. EMP doesn't do the job inside a body. But this does." Keller held up the weapon that was glowing hot. He casually tossed it into the hole. "Your love of old S22s was your downfall. But you didn't know about the blind spot that can allow a boarding attack through a laser cut point. This one was the only one to notice." He kicked Jade's body. "Soon, you'll be dead, and everyone will think I am, too. You made sure of that. But I'll have new flesh because I'm immortal like Ty. Yes, I'm a New Jovian soldier. But better."

Cobb threw the rifle at Keller and then launched up and over the REAPER. To land directly inside an escape pod. He hammered the launch button with his heel, the hatch slammed, and it launched.

My god…Kira, Jade, Lita, Elza…

Chapter 28: The Least of Them

Jade regained consciousness slowly to the sounds of straining engines. She was face down in a pool of her own blood. She knew her nose must be broken. She soon discovered trying to sit up that her left arm had a fracture in either her ulna or radius bones, or both.

She struggled to sit up. She nearly vomited as she did. Elza, Kira, and Lita's headless bodies lay on the cargo floor at her feet. A lake of blood surrounded them.

She gritted her jaw to struggle to her knees as her tongue found a broken tooth.

Jade started to laugh. She knew she would seem insane if anyone were watching. Maybe she was. She drew her knife and got to what needed doing.

When Keller returned to the cargo bay, Jade was on her feet. She had a makeshift sling made of a small green duffel bag across her chest. Jade stood in the center of the cargo bay in a lake of blood. The lower half of her face was bloody, as was her right arm, up to the elbow.

Keller laughed at her as she struggled with one slick hand to bring the rifle to bear. She was staggering.

"I've killed the rest, and the least of them remains. You must have seen by now that I'm immortal, and your pesky rifle, even with armor-piercing rounds, will do nothing." Keller laughed again. "Nothing to say, little kitten?"

"Nothing to say to you, Asswipe." Jade spat out the tooth. "But to Cobb… Sorry about your ship." Her helmet snapped closed.

She fired the Grendel.

Keller, the REAPER, parked in the cargo bay of the *TULSA* 471, and the entire ship before her was gone that instant. So was the Grendel, taking Jade's right arm below the elbow with it.

When she regained consciousness, she was tumbling in space. A strobe was flashing in her peripheral vision. Or was this what happened with this much pain? The severed half of the *TULSA*'s cargo bay tumbled a hundred meters away. She could see her arm was gone at the elbow, but the advanced vac-suit she wore automatically cinched down a tourniquet on the arm.

Too bad, I could have bled out faster otherwise and be done. No regrets. We got him.

The moon came closer as the darkness closed in…

"Jade. It's time to wake up, sweetheart." A voice intruded on the bliss of oblivion.

Mom, is that you? I must be dead.

"Jade. We have fresh coffee…" a second voice said.

"I fucking hate coffee…" Jade whispered through a dry throat.

Another voice said, "Coffee won't work on her like it did with Cobb. Lower the light to 50%."

Someone forced first one eye open, then the other, and flashed a blinding light to see her brain. Jade tried to bat the torturer away, but she was a ghost and had no hand.

"Slow and steady, the nanites won't let her fever go above 102F but will bring her out."

Her eyes were watering now, a faint sizzle of nanites in her ears. She naturally blinked, and the tears ran down her neck. She opened her eyes, blinking.

"There she is," her mother said.

"Am I dead?" Jade asked, then grimaced at the pain.

"Nope. Nice try, though," a brunette said.

Now, both women were standing on either side of her. She watched the rest of the auto-doc retract around her as it began to sit her up. To face her father.

"Here, drink this water." He brought a straw to her mouth. She sipped a bit. It helped.

She looked down at herself. Her left arm was in a clear, inflated cast. From her fingers to her biceps, her entire arm was black, blue, and green.

Her right arm was gone below the elbow.

"Where am I? Who are you people?" Jade demanded. "What have you done to me?"

"You did this to yourself, Jade," a blond woman said gently. "It amazes me that they can replace our entire bodies faster than they can put you back in working order."

"Elza? Lita?" Jade knew them by the eyes. Kira took her left hand and gave her fingers a slight squeeze. Elza stroked her right shoulder.

Now, real tears began to flow. From them all.

"You saved us," Lita said through the tears.

"From an eternity of darkness," Elza said. "We owe you more than our lives."

Jade held up the stump for a look. "It was a fair trade."

Lita laughed, and Elza kissed her forehead.

"Mom, Dad? How are you here? I saw the farm." Jade cried harder.

"We were deep in the caverns when the strike hit. The orbot Cobb assigned us was destroyed, but Hunter could find us when we got the orb into another socket."

The door slid open to several shouting voices. Cobb stormed in with several doctors in tow, trailing wires and IV lines behind him.

A single gaze from Jade's eyes somehow silenced all the doctors at once. The white of her eyes were now blood red from her injuries.

"Hey, Cobb," Jade said. "Sorry about the ship."

"I'd trade that ship for you any day of the week," Cobb said as loud footsteps in the hall sent people scattering.

Ty walked in. All his flesh was gone again. He wore no coveralls. He was all combat chassis.

"Hi, handsome," Lita said to Ty.

"Soon…" was Ty's reply.

"Where are we? What happened?" Jade asked.

Cobb replied. "We're currently in the *WINTHROP* hospital ring in orbit over Pratt."

"When you fired the Grendel in space, it generated a massive gravity wave that traveled at the speed of light, spreading as it went. The *HOLLAND* was several parsecs away but easily detected it. Your suit's distress beacon and strobe allowed him to pick you, Elza, Kira, and Lita up first. Ty was next. He made an impressive crater, I understand."

Ty nodded.

"I was not so lucky," Cobb said quickly. "The escape pod was damaged in the gravity wave. I barely survived."

"My ship?" Jade asked.

"Coe picked up Ty in your ship. Then, he flew it to my crash sight. We got you into a stasis pod on the *HOLLAND* until they could get you back to the *WINTHROP*. No one knew then that you'd... saved Elza, Kira, and Lita."

Everyone then realized Jade had cut the orbs out of all the bodies. The conversations lagged.

"Who do I have to kill to get some food around here?" Jade said.

Michael Frost poked his head into the room just then. "Hey, guys! It's Taco Tuesday!" and disappeared.

Jade's broken nose was repaired, but she still had two black eyes. More drastically, the whites of her eyes were still completely red. Plates and screws had been required to reassemble all the bone fragments in her shattered left arm, but the nanites had healed the flesh enough that she could use her left hand without too many restrictions.

One of the Frost brothers carried her tray to the table, where a seat was reserved for her at the end. Kira was last to arrive. She carried a box with her but didn't mention it as she set it down and went to get in line for tacos.

Jade ate awkwardly with one hand, hunger overriding embarrassment.

When everyone was done, all the Frost brothers cleared the trays and dishes without being asked.

Kira set the box on the table before Jade and said, "Happy birthday."

"It's not my birthday," Jade replied.

"Just shut up and open it," Kira said.

Why was everyone smiling?

It was a right arm. It looked real. But the lined socket gave it away.

"It's from my own collection," Kira said. "Easily modified."

Jade lifted it with her left hand from the box by the wrist.

"The doctors already updated the control nanites in your deep brain implant suite," Kira said. "Think. Concentrate. Imagine your hand was still there."

The fingers moved. Jade's eyes went wide.

"That'll be… handy," Allan Frost said, deadpan.

As everyone groaned at the pun, the hand slowly made a fist and then raised its middle finger toward Frost.

Cobb shook his head and decided to spend another night in the auto-doc.

Chapter 29: Aftermath

"We're going back to Lumina Station," Lita said. "Fresh start. Ty has a standing job offer from Sec Chief Boone there. We have friends there. We'll try to live our next lifetime without murdering so many people who deserve it. Well, not too many, hopefully."

"You're not flying that little four-seater all that way, are you?" Jade asked, hugging Lita.

"No way, Cruze is dropping us off in her fancy ship," Lita said.

"Cruze's navigator Pots and I had a long chat yesterday. I like her," Jade said.

"Thanks for bringing her back to me," Ty said in his rumbling baritone. She felt the words in his chest as he hugged her.

"You're welcome." Jade looked at Lita. "It was my honor to be able to do so."

"Just so you know, Ty always stops hugging last," Lita said. Jade knew it was because he had his flesh back. Again.

Kira, Cobb, and Elza had already said their goodbyes but showed up to wave as they boarded.

"So, Cobb, how did you manage to keep so many of your original parts?" Jade asked as they walked her to the hatch.

"It's because I'm so ruggedly handsome," Cobb said, and he immediately received pokes in the ribs.

"Cobbal Block?" Cobb heard a threat in that voice behind him. Then he heard a gun clatter to the floor before he could turn around. When he did turn, Jade had a man by the throat up against the bulkhead.

Jade turned to Cobb with a raised eyebrow. Cobb shrugged. "Call him Cobb…" Jade crushed his spine with her cyborg grip.

"Have security clean this up," Cobb said. "Elza and Hunter can question him later."

"Holy shit, Jade," Kira said. "When did you turn savage?"

Jade took a moment to think.

When indeed. Am I savage? Am I the Jade that arrived here just a few months ago? Both I think…

"Taco Tuesday, maybe. When I ran out of fucks to give."

AFTERWARD

In the year of 2024, I got back on track. 2023 was a challenging year for me that really set me back on my writing efforts. In separate monkey wrench events: I crashed my mountain bike resulting in a shattered collar bone, a dislocated shoulder and two broken ribs. Later in the summer, I had a heart attack, complete with a 99% blockage of the right coronary artery, emergency surgery, and a shiny new stent. All of that really cut into my writing time.

With the encouragement of fellow authors and friends S.C. Megale and David Keener, I got back on track in Q4 of 2023.

I have ambitious goals for 2024. I hope to publish this novel on March 31, 2024. If the schedule holds, it may be the most I have published in a single year.

Wish me luck.

Plus, I finally got a dog. Her name's Whiskey. I can't believe I waited so long. She keep walking…

Martin Wilsey
Fredericksburg, VA
March 17, 2024

ABOUT THE AUTHOR

Mr. Wilsey's first novel, *Still Falling*, was published on March 31st, 2015. Less than three years he retired from his career as a research scientist for a government-funded think tank. As a full-time author, Mr. Wilsey still uses his research and whiteboard skills to keep the books flowing. He likes to put science back into science fiction.

Mr. Wilsey has more projects than time, so please feel free to email him and distract him even more.

He and his wife, Brenda, live in Virginia with their pets, Whiskey, Brandy, and Bailey.

Email him or follow him on social media!

He just might kill you in his next novel...

ACKNOWLEDGMENTS

Many people have helped and encouraged me with this book. To begin with, I would like to thank Jessica and Larry Bright for all their support and for allowing me to use their cottage for a Writer Retreat. The peace and lack of distractions let me crank out the first draft of this book in twelve days. Thank you so much. You will get the first signed copy!

Many others have helped me and deserve my thanks: Erica Gravely, Kelly Lenz Carr, Joe Kirk, Ron Jennings, Travis Beck, Lea Jones, and Donna Royston.

I also need to thank the Loudoun Science Fiction and Fantasy Writers Group, aka The Hourlings, for helping me become a better writer and distracting me with projects I can't resist. Especially S.C. Megale and David Keener for pushing me and keeping me on track, realistic, and humble.

A special thanks to my wife, Brenda, for all the help and support she brings me.

I must also thank, as usual, my cat, Bailey. He doesn't care if I ever sell another book as long as the sun shines on his window seat as I write. My new dog Whiskey will keep me walking, and maybe she'll appear in one of my novels in the future.

FOR MORE INFORMATION:

https://linktr.ee/wilsey
martin.wilsey@gmail.com

To see all the titles by Martin Wilsey, scan this code:

Coming Soon from

Martin Wilsey

Coming Soon from

Martin Wilsey

Coming Soon from

Martin Wilsey

Coming Soon from

Martin Wilsey

www.ingramcontent.com/pod-product-compliance
Lightning Source LLC
Chambersburg PA
CBHW072028220726

48293CB00016B/548